J-FICTION

THE MENA

HE GERIE

TUI T. SUTHERLAND
KARI SUTHERLAND

HARPER

An Imprint of HarperCollins*Publishers*

The Menagerie
Copyright © 2013 by Tui T. Sutherland and Kari Sutherland
Map art by Ali Solomon
All rights reserved. Printed in the United States of America.
No part of this book may be used or reproduced in any manner
whatsoever without written permission except in the case of
brief quotations embodied in critical articles and reviews.
For information address HarperCollins Children's Books,
a division of HarperCollins Publishers, 10 East 53rd Street,
New York, NY 10022.
www.harpercollinschildrens.com

Library of Congress Cataloging-in-Publication Data
is available.
ISBN 978-0-06-078064-7

Typography by Torborg Davern
13 14 15 16 17   CG/RRDH   10 9 8 7 6 5 4 3 2 1
❖
First Edition

For Adam, Steve, Elliot, and Jonah,
for whom we'd happily brave dragons,
kelpies, and griffins. As for manticores, you
might be on your own there.

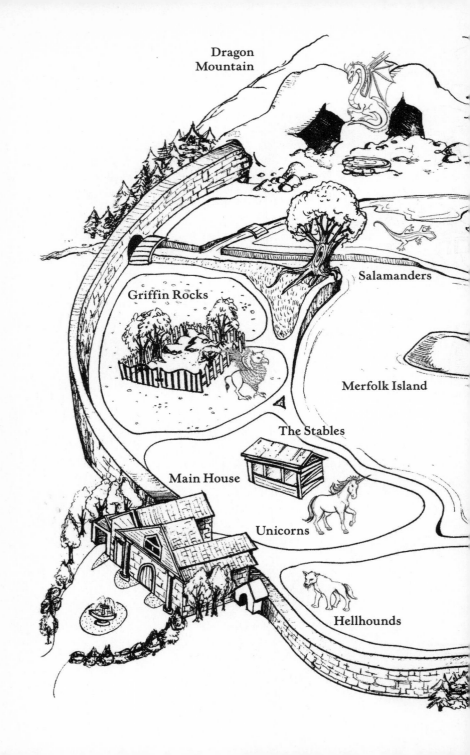

Dragon
Mountain

Salamanders

Griffin Rocks

Merfolk Island

The Stables

Main House

Unicorns

Hellhounds

Mammoth

Reptile House

Yeti
Highalnds

Zaratan

Aviary

Kraken Cove

Phoenix

Dark Forest

Baku

ONE

L ogan Wilde noticed the feathers as soon as he woke up. There were five of them scattered across his gray carpet like autumn leaves. Logan stared at them, rubbing his eyes as his third backup alarm clock went off.

He climbed out of bed and picked one up. It was huge, and in the sunlight it glowed as if it were sprinkled with gold dust, bright against the pale brown of his palm.

He tried to remember if anything weird had happened last night, such as, say, a giant golden bird flapping through his room. The problem was that he was a really, *really* deep sleeper. His dad joked that he could set off a car alarm beside Logan's head without waking him up.

"Huh," Logan said. "Do I want to know what happened to the rest of this bird, Purrsimmon?"

He turned and noticed that his cat wasn't lounging sleepily across the bottom of his bed, where he could usually find her.

"Purrs?" he called.

A movement on Logan's desk caught his eye. Warrior, his Siamese fighting fish, was swimming frantically back and forth, swishing his long purple fins. The terrarium next to the fishbowl looked empty. Logan crossed over to it and peered in.

Normally his two pet mice ran up to the glass when they saw him, hoping for food. But today Mr. and Mrs. Smith were huddled in a corner under a pile of wood shavings. They refused to come out even when he shook their food canister at them.

"What the heck is going on?" Logan asked.

"Rrreow," said a small voice from inside the closet.

Logan pulled open the door and found his cat hiding on the top shelf behind a pile of sweaters. Her gray and white fur was standing on end, and she gave him a wild-eyed look.

"Aw, what happened?" Logan joked. "Did a big bird fly in here and scare you?"

"Rrrrrreeow," she grumbled. Her baleful glare said, *Well, YOU clearly weren't going to wake up and save us. Go ahead, snore away while I get eaten. I'm sure your tears at my funeral will be very heartfelt.*

Logan spotted long threads of blue, green, and red yarn tangled through her claws and realized that Purrsimmon had spent the night anxiously shredding his sweaters.

"Oh, man," Logan said. "Thanks a lot, Purrs."

"*RRRRREOW*," she protested indignantly. He reached for her, but she flattened her ears and took a flying leap over his head. He spun around in time to see her tail disappearing out the open window.

Logan sighed. "Someday I'll have a dog," he told his fish. "One that won't run away in a panic over every little thing."

Warrior flapped his fins at Logan as if he were saying, *Hey, I'm on the cat's side here!*

Logan got dressed, picked up the note and lunch money his dad had left for him in the kitchen, and hurried out the door, grabbing a Pop-Tart to eat on the way to school.

It never occurred to him that his nighttime visitor might not have left.

Xanadu, Wyoming, was a small, sleepy town surrounded by mountains. It was not the kind of place Logan had ever expected to live. But then, he'd also never expected his mom to ditch them via postcard or his dad to quit his fancy lawyer job to move west and search for her.

"Look at this place, Dad," Logan had said that summer as their U-Haul bumped past what appeared to be an actual saloon, with a pair of long horns burned into a wooden sign.

"It's like the opposite of Chicago. Does this mean I can have a horse? I bet everyone here has a horse."

"Sure, you can have a horse," his dad answered, "the day you go to school wearing a cowboy hat, chaps, and spurs."

Dad thought he was pretty hilarious.

Logan wasn't nearly brave enough for a cowboy hat, never mind anything else. Certainly not as the new kid in seventh grade.

It would be pretty cool to ride a horse the ten minutes to school instead of his bike, though. Logan coasted down a hill, steering around the potholes. He still missed the deep-dish pizza smell that hung around his block in Chicago, but he didn't miss most of the other smells of the city. The air here smelled like pine trees and faraway snow.

At the bottom of the hill, his bike zipped past the Xanadu Savings Bank. He spotted a cluster of people in suits on the front steps. He didn't have time to stop, but out of the corner of his eye, it looked as if the front door had been shredded like grated cheese.

No way. I must have seen that wrong. Logan shook his head and kept pedaling.

Logan liked Wyoming better than Chicago so far, even if he hadn't made any real friends yet. People actually did ride horses down the main streets sometimes, and the town newsletter was printed—not online—in an old-timey font like a Wanted: Dead or Alive outlaw poster. In Wyoming

Logan had an actual yard—well, a strip of grass around the patio of their ranch house—which meant there was hope that one day he could have a dog. The best part was that his dad let him bike around alone.

Plus, here there weren't memories of his mom, waiting to ambush him everywhere he looked. He couldn't imagine why his dad thought he'd find her anywhere nearby. Xanadu was way too dull for her; there wasn't even an airport within fifty miles. Logan didn't mind the quiet, but his mom would have lost her mind in the first week.

He rounded the last corner and nearly crashed into a trio of kids standing in the middle of the road, arguing.

"AAAAAH!" he shouted, steering wildly as two of the kids scattered. His bike rammed into the curb and sent him sprawling into a pile of raked orange leaves on someone's lawn.

"Watch where you're going!" a girl's voice yelled.

"Me?" Logan said, sitting up. "You're the ones standing in the street!" His elbow ached, and his palms were scraped. He could feel a thin trickle of blood sliding down his shin. He unclipped his bike helmet and leaned over to roll up his pants.

The girl who had yelled at him was still standing in the road, glaring. She was the only one who hadn't tried to move out of the way. Her dark hair hung down in two long braids. He realized he'd noticed her before, yelling at another sixth-grade girl on the soccer field; but he didn't know her name. The other two were in his seventh-grade class.

"Whoa," said the guy, squinting at Logan's bleeding knee. "Sorry about that." Blue Merevy was tall and blond and sleepy looking. Girls were always smiling at him and hanging around wherever he was. Logan wasn't sure why, although it probably had something to do with his green eyes and the really slow way he talked.

"It's all right," Logan said. He glanced at the other girl— Zoe Kahn, the weirdest person in the seventh grade. Her chin-length red-brown hair was tucked behind her ears, and her green flannel shirt was buttoned wrong. She was staring across the street at the post office, frowning.

"Keiko," she said as if Logan wasn't there, "come on, please. We need your help."

"No way," Keiko said, tossing her braids back. "Stupid thing will probably bite me if it sees me. This is your problem. I'm staying out of it." She narrowed her gold-brown eyes at Logan, then whirled around and stomped off toward the school.

"We're going to be late," Blue pointed out.

"But we have to check," Zoe said desperately. "What if he's gone by lunchtime?"

"It'll be all right," Blue said, lowering his voice.

Logan felt like he was intruding. He climbed to his feet and was about to slink off, but then he glanced at Zoe's face again and noticed that she was on the verge of tears. Even Blue looked kind of stressed, which was not a normal Blue expression at all.

He'd feel like a jerk if he walked away without asking if he could help. "Is everything okay?"

"Yeah, it's nothing," Zoe said, swiping at her eyes.

"You sure?" he asked. "Is, uh—is there anything I can do?"

Zoe met his gaze for the first time, as if she'd finally realized he was there. "Oh, thanks," she said, "but no, it's okay. It's just my—my dog is missing."

"Oh, no!" Logan said. "What kind of dog? How long has he been gone? What's his name? Did you check the shelter? I can help you make flyers if you want. Is he microchipped? Has he run away before?" He stopped. Blue and Zoe were both giving him very strange looks. "Um," he said. "I like dogs, that's all."

"Don't worry about it," Zoe said. She gave him a tired smile. "But thanks."

The warning bell rang in the school yard.

"We'd better go, quick," Zoe said to Blue. She dashed across the street and disappeared into the post office. Logan noticed a few feathers scattered across the big stone steps— enormous feathers like the ones in his room, only these were dark brown instead of gold.

"Why would her dog be in there?" Logan asked.

"Uh . . . he *really* loves mailmen." Blue shrugged. "He's kind of a weird dog."

"What's his name?"

Blue's forehead furrowed thoughtfully. "Uh . . . Six. No, Finn. Nah, let's go with Six. See ya." He turned to follow Zoe before Logan could ask any more questions, such as "Did you just really obviously make that up?"

Logan sighed as Blue disappeared through the post office doors. This was why he still didn't have any friends four months after moving to Xanadu. It wasn't only that he was totally awkward when he tried to talk to people. And it wasn't that he looked different from almost everyone here—Walter Barnes, the other African American guy in the class, was a mega-popular football star with an eighth-grade girlfriend.

The truth was, the kids here already had their set groups of friends. There were only twenty-four students in the whole seventh grade—ten boys, fourteen girls—and all of them were impossible to get to know.

The first week, he had tried sitting with Walter at lunch. But Walter had ignored him, talking to his football buddies and acting as if his lasagna was far more interesting than Logan. He didn't seem to care about the Bulls or the Cubs or how many games Logan had gone to in Chicago.

Logan had tried a different table of guys the next week, hoping that he'd have better luck with the band guys than the jocks since he was a decent saxophone player. But when he brought up Charlie Parker, he got blank stares. Nobody liked the same things he did. None of them had ever watched

MythBusters or *The Amazing Race.* As for Siamese fighting fish, he might as well have said he kept a small, boring alien in a fishbowl on his desk.

They spent most of lunch quoting old *South Park* episodes to one another, which was a show Logan's dad wouldn't let him watch. After that, Logan kept sitting at the same table, but he stopped trying to participate in the conversations.

Basically it was hopeless. But his friends back in Chicago hadn't been that awesome, either. They all said cheesy, unhelpful things when his mom left and then didn't want to talk about it. And from their two-sentence emails, it sounded like he was lucky to be missing all the middle school drama of who liked whom and who was sending around embarrassing pictures of whom. Here he might be invisible, but at least he wasn't in everyone's in-box squirting grape juice out of his nose.

He slouched into homeroom and drew feathers on the inside of his notebook until the bell rang. Mr. Christopher was just starting to take attendance when Zoe and Blue were escorted through the door by an irate guidance counselor.

"These two were playing hooky!" Miss McCaffrey announced, then paused dramatically before adding, "In the POST OFFICE!" as if that made it much, much worse.

"Oooooooooooooooo," said Jasmin Sterling from the back of the room. "Zoe and Blue, sending each other love letters! That's soooo cute."

Blue's mellow expression didn't change, but Zoe shot her

a withering look. Everybody, even Logan, knew that Jasmin was the one with the world's biggest crush on Blue. Zoe and Blue acted more like brother and sister, at least as far as he could tell.

The overhead loudspeaker crackled. "Miss McCaffrey," said the disembodied voice of the principal, "please report to the cafeteria. We have a . . . situation."

Zoe gave Blue a frantic look as the guidance counselor went out the door. Logan saw Blue shake his head a tiny bit and nudge her toward her seat.

Zoe slid into the chair beside Logan, running her hands anxiously through her hair. She dropped her backpack on the floor between her desk and Logan's. He wondered if she knew how peculiar her bag smelled. It was as if wet dogs and hippos had been wrestling on it. He glanced down and saw a couple of brown hairs stuck in the zipper. They were too long and dark to be Zoe's; her hair was more reddish and barely reached her chin. So they must belong to her dog, which meant he was shaggy with a bizarre odor.

Well, he'd rather have a dog with a bizarre odor than no dog. Logan tried to think what kind of dog would have fur like that. A Saint Bernard?

Blue's desk was in front of Logan's. His thick blond hair had a slight greenish tint to it that Logan had only noticed because the back of Blue's head was right in front of him all day long. He also had an odd smell—like the sea, as if he spent most of the day surfing, although there weren't any beaches for hundreds of miles.

Mr. Christopher turned to the blackboard and began writing out a math problem. A crumpled ball of paper zipped past Logan's nose and bonked Blue on the back of the head.

Blue and Logan both turned to Zoe at the same time.

"We have to get to the cafeteria," she whispered, ignoring Logan.

Blue nodded at Mr. Christopher's back. "But we have class."

Zoe rubbed her thin wrist. "This is more important! You know what SNAPA'll do if we don't find—" She stopped and glanced at Logan.

"What's Snapple got to do with your dog?" he asked.

"Um," she said. "Nothing. I didn't say that. We need to know what's happening," she whispered to Blue, sounding frustrated.

"He won't let you go," Blue said, shaking his head. "Or me. Not after we were late like that."

Logan knew that if it were *his* dog, he'd be just as desperate as Zoe sounded right now. For his own dog, he'd do anything to get it back.

"I'll go," he whispered, raising his hand.

TWO

"Wait, no," Zoe objected, but the teacher was already looking at him.

"Mr. Christopher? May I go to the bathroom?" Logan asked.

His teacher put down the chalk and sighed. "All right, but no loitering," he said, pulling out the hall pass.

Logan glanced back from the door and saw Zoe biting her thumbnail nervously. "Don't worry," he mouthed.

The hallway was empty as he hurried toward the cafeteria, past rows of yellow lockers. He could hear raised voices as he got closer. He stopped outside the green metal double doors and crouched down, pretending to tie his shoe while he listened.

"How could it *all* be gone?" cried Miss McCaffrey.

"There's nothing left!" That was the voice of Buck, the man who ran the cafeteria kitchen. "I'm telling you, something got into the freezer *and* the refrigerator and ate it all. The chili, the taco shells, the cheese, the Jell-O, the chocolate milk, the chopped tomatoes—everything we were going to serve for lunch today! Gone!"

"It must have been a wild animal," said Principal Upton in his drawling, half-asleep voice. "Maybe a bear."

"A very neat bear," Buck pointed out. "One that could open doors and cans."

"Cans?" said Miss McCaffrey.

"Look!" said Buck. "All the baked beans. Pried open and licked clean!"

"Maybe the bear used its claws," said the principal doubtfully.

"It left nothing but the lettuce." Buck sounded mournful. "And these red feathers. It must have brought some kind of bird in here to eat it."

"Well, we can't serve lettuce for lunch!" Miss McCaffrey snapped.

"I know that!" Buck shouted.

"Don't you throw feathers at me!" she yelled.

"Mr. Wilde?"

Logan jumped a mile. He'd completely forgotten about

pretending to tie his shoe, or watching for anyone coming along the hall.

The school librarian was standing over him, looking friendly and puzzled. She had caramel-colored skin and long, wispy black hair pulled back in a ponytail. Her ankle-length skirt was bright green with tiny diamond-shaped mirrors sewn all over it, and her blouse was a rather startlingly mismatched shade of bright pink. He couldn't remember her name. He was pretty astonished that she knew his.

"Oh, uh, sorry," he said, scrambling to his feet. "I was— I was just—"

She put one finger to her lips. "Have they figured it out?" she whispered, nodding at the cafeteria door.

He shook his head.

"Have *you* figured it out?" she asked.

"Me?" he said. "I don't know anything. I'm just tying my shoe."

"Hmmm," she said, glancing skeptically at his sneakers. "Did they say something about feathers?"

"Yeah, but it couldn't have been a bird. Birds don't eat chili," Logan said. "I mean—right?" She was staring into the cafeteria as if she wasn't really listening.

"Go on, shoo," she said, waving at him. Relieved, he fled down the hall.

Mr. Christopher was giving a speech about polynomials when Logan got back, so he slipped into his seat and tore a piece of paper out of his notebook.

Something ate all the food in the cafeteria, he wrote. *Doesn't sound like it could have been a dog, though. Maybe a bear? Nothing much happening now, just grown-ups shouting.* He folded the note, and when Mr. Christopher wasn't looking, he tossed it onto Zoe's desk.

She read it, groaned softly, and clunked her head down on her folded arms. Which wasn't the reaction he'd been expecting.

Logan concentrated on picking loose scraps of paper out of his notebook's spiral binding. It wasn't like he really needed to be friends with weird Zoe Kahn anyway. She was constantly falling asleep in class and making up wild stories about why her homework wasn't done. Even if the teacher couldn't tell she was lying, Logan could.

Her clothes were always ripped or stained, and she acted like she didn't even care. She mumbled to herself and bit her nails and looked worried all the time. She barely spoke to anyone but Blue, who was mysteriously friends with her even though he could have hung out with anyone.

Logan didn't need a friend *that* badly. Did he?

It was a relief to get home after a long day of boring classes and boring lunch, most of which he spent thinking about places in Xanadu where a dog might hide. He wheeled his bike into the garage and let himself into the house.

"Purrs?" he called.

"*Rrrreow,*" she answered from under the couch.

"Still acting crazy?" he asked, grabbing a Gatorade from the kitchen. "Boy, something really spooked you, didn't it?"

"RRRRRRRRRRREOW."

There was another note from his dad on the kitchen counter. *Busy work weekend ahead,* it said. *Sorry I'll be out so much. Pizza and the Bears game Sunday night? Lots of leftovers in the fridge when you get hungry. Call if you need me.*

Logan knew his dad's new job with the wildlife department kept him busy, and he liked that his dad trusted him to be on his own. But he was pretty sure some of those extra "work" hours were actually spent searching for Mom. After all, the last postcard from her—all lame excuses and good-byes—had been mailed from Cheyenne, Wyoming. It wasn't a coincidence that Dad had suddenly moved them here a month after it arrived. They never talked about it, but obviously Dad was hoping to find her and change her mind.

That wasn't going to happen, though. His mom had always liked traveling more than being at home. She'd barely slowed down to eat dinner even when she *was* home. She wasn't the kind of mom who was into family game nights and bike rides, even if she loved Logan and his dad. Logan had always felt like she had a duffel bag packed and ready to go, so he shouldn't have been surprised or hurt when she finally didn't come back.

He was, though.

Who broke up with their family by postcard?

Still, lots of his friends in Chicago had only one parent. For most of them it was the dad who'd left and the mom who'd stayed. Or the dad who'd never been there in the first place. Or the dad who was there but acted more like an extra couch cushion than a person.

So really, Logan was lucky. At least he had a dad who made burritos and shot hoops with him in the driveway and tried to read the same books Logan did.

He shook his head. He didn't want to think about this.

"Okay, Purrs," he said, "I'm going to feed Mr. and Mrs. Smith, if you want to come watch." Normally Purrsimmon loved to sit on his desk and stare ominously at his mice while Logan fed them. But today she refused to come out from under the couch.

With a shrug, Logan went into his room, dropped his backpack, and checked on the mouse cage. Mr. and Mrs. Smith were still huddled under their pile of wood shavings. Their small pink noses twitched at him anxiously.

"Poor little guys," Logan said, picking up their food container. "What's got you so—" He paused. "That's weird." The container felt much lighter than it had that morning. He pulled off the top of the canister and peered inside.

It was completely empty.

"What the . . . ," Logan muttered. "Guys, who ate all

your food?" *And then put the lid back on?*

"SQUUUUUUUUUUOOOOOOOOOOOOOOORP."

Logan froze. That was a noise he had definitely never heard before. And it had come from somewhere in his room.

He turned around slowly, his heart pounding.

That's when he saw the tail stretched out along his carpet, sticking out from the trailing edge of his comforter. A long, golden, furry lion's tail.

There was a monster under his bed.

THREE

It couldn't be a lion. There weren't any lions in Wyoming. Right? Maybe cougars, but those didn't have tails like that.

Logan grabbed the baseball bat that was leaning inside his closet door. Cautiously he edged a bit closer, then crouched down and peered under the bed.

The thing had its eyes closed. The front half of it looked like a giant golden eagle, wings and beak and all. The rest of its body was furry, with sharp lion claws on its four paws.

A bolt of fear shot through him, followed immediately by relief. It wasn't real. It couldn't be real. Something else must have made the noise. And this must be some kind of weird stuffed animal his grandparents had sent for him. Sometimes

Grams forgot that twelve-year-olds wanted iPods and video games and dogs, not kid toys.

But what kind of animal was a bird at one end and a lion on the other? He'd never seen a stuffed toy like that before.

Well, whatever it was, at least he could be sure that it was absolutely, one hundred percent not real.

The creature's eyes popped open.

"Mork!" it declared.

Logan slammed backward into the closet door and dropped the baseball bat. It was alive! He was about to be eaten by a . . . by a lion-eagle thing!

"Mork!" the creature warbled again, clacking its beak at him. At least it didn't *sound* threatening. In fact, the noises it made were kind of cute. "Mork! Mork!"

"I'm asleep," Logan said. "I'm dreaming. I'm hallucinating."

"Mork!" the thing under the bed insisted. "MORK!"

Logan closed his eyes. "Logan, you're imagining this. There must have been something weird in the pizzas they got us for lunch. There is definitely not a monster under your bed morking at you right now."

Loooooooogan!

Was that a voice inside his head? Logan peeked. The creature's eyes were dark and huge, watching him with bright curiosity. They looked exactly the way he'd always imagined his future dog's eyes would look.

"Was that you?" Logan asked.

Logan hear me?

"Um—" Logan started.

"Mork!"

His bed shuddered and shifted as the animal slowly crawled out into the open and Logan got his first good look at it. It was smaller than he'd thought—no bigger than a Labrador puppy. Soft golden wings unfurled from its furry back. Long lion claws dug into his gray carpet as it shook itself, lion tail lashing. The feathers on its head and chest blurred into fur for the rest of its body. Its hooked beak went *clack clack clack* as it snapped at the air. A crest of golden feathers fanned out around its head like a tiny mane.

Logan realized he had seen a drawing of something like this before, on the cover of a Diana Wynne Jones fantasy book. It looked like a griffin . . . but those didn't exist.

It shook itself again and bounded over to him. Before he could scramble away, it leaped into his lap. He winced as its claws sank through his jeans, but it didn't attack. It tucked its tail around itself and sat down. Its dark eyes stared at him earnestly, and when it head-butted his chest, he couldn't resist reaching out to pat it.

"Mooooooork," the creature gurgled in delight, wriggling closer to him and curling into a ball just like his cat. Logan stroked its soft fur—even softer than Purrsimmon's—and carefully touched one of its folded wings. This didn't feel like a dream or a pizza-induced hallucination.

"What the heck are you?" he asked. "Some kind of government experiment?" Scientists were always putting plants together and making weird fruits like pluots, after all. Maybe they could make eaglions as well.

The creature opened its mouth, but instead of saying "Mork" again, it let out a loud "SQUUOOORP."

Logan laughed. "So may I call you Squorp?" he asked.

Squorp! chirped the voice in his head. **Good name! Squorp like Squorp! Logan! Listening!**

"That's right," Logan said. "I'm Logan. You're Squorp."

Squorp eat! It nipped at one of Logan's fingers, and he pulled his hand away with a yelp.

"Okay, but not me!" he said. "You're the one who ate all the mouse food, aren't you?"

Squorp hungry, said the creature, giving him the saddest eyes an eagle face could muster. **Small scritchy food very very gross.** Its face brightened. **Eat small scritchies instead?**

"No," Logan said sternly. It was lucky the lid on his terrarium was locked down to protect Mr. and Mrs. Smith from Purrsimmon. "No eating my mice. They're my friends."

Squorp nestled closer to him and leaned his head on Logan's chest. **Squorp your friend.**

"Aww," Logan said, scratching Squorp's head.

Squorp much better friend than small scritchies. Small scritchies unnecessary. And delicious!

"NO," Logan said. "We'll get you hamburger instead. Okay? You'll like that much better, I promise."

Suddenly Squorp bolted upright and clacked his beak frantically. **Uh-oh!** The little creature leaped onto Logan's bed and burrowed into the bedclothes, shedding golden fur all over his sheets.

"What?" Logan asked, standing up. "What happened?"

"Mork!" Squorp yelped. With a frantic glance at the window, he rolled and dug the sheets around until he was just a big lump under the dark blue comforter.

Logan peeked out the window, then ducked quickly out of sight.

Zoe and Blue were standing right outside, staring at the low hedges around his house.

FOUR

"More feathers!" Zoe's anxious voice floated through the window. "That's all we're ever going to find. Maybe this *is* my fault. SNAPA's going to shut us down and Dad will ground me for life and everyone will have to be relocated and I'll never see you or Captain Fuzzbutt or Mooncrusher ever again."

"On the plus side, maybe they'll send Keiko back to Japan," said Blue.

"This isn't funny, Blue!" Zoe paused. "Well, okay, that would be the one upside."

"We don't know it's your fault," Blue said kindly. "And it's not so bad. No SNAPA officials are out hunting them yet, and we haven't seen any wildlife guys stomping around investigating. We just have to find them all before Sunday."

Them? Logan glanced at the Squorp-shaped lump on his bed.

"Why aren't you more worried?" Zoe asked. "If SNAPA shuts us down, who knows what'll happen to your dad. Or where they might make you live."

There was that word again. *Snappa, not Snapple,* Logan thought.

Blue shrugged. "I only worry about things that have actually happened. If I started worrying about all the things that *might* happen, I'd be . . . well, I'd be you."

"Yeah, thanks," Zoe said. She sighed. "This one must be long gone."

"Let's check in at home," Blue said.

"Okay," said Zoe, sounding defeated. "I still have to do my chores anyway. But if any of them are spotted . . ."

"I know," Blue said. "It'll be the end of the world. Again."

Logan heard them pick up their bikes and pedal away. His head was spinning.

Squorp poked his beak out from under the covers. **Worry-Cub gone?** his voice warbled in Logan's head.

"Worry-Cub?"

Only a cub, but worries and worries and double-checks and worries more. Always flapping her paws but not trying to fly. Probably losing her fur. Bites her claws, too.

That sounded like Zoe, all right.

"Squorp," Logan said. "*You're* Zoe's dog!"

The griffin threw off the comforter and ruffled his tawny feathers into an indignant fluff on his chest. **Squorp no such thing! Muscles and Killer and Jaws and Sheldon all dogs! Captain Fuzzbutt all Zoe's! Squorp neither Zoe's NOR dog! Squorp all mine own and ALL GRIFFIN!**

"Well, okay," Logan said. "But you're the thing she's looking for. Aren't you?"

Squorp studied his talons intently. **Ohhhh, only one of them.**

"How many others are there?" Logan asked.

The griffin squirmed. **Two brothers and three sisters.** He swiveled his head around as if he expected them to pop out of the closet. **Miss them! Well, most of them. Not Clink. She bossy.**

"Six griffins wandering around Xanadu? No wonder Zoe's freaking out," Logan said. He leaned over his computer and typed *snappa* into Google, hoping for a clue. "I bet that's even worse than losing a dog. Man, I shouldn't have let them leave all upset like that. We have to get you home."

Noooooo! Squorp flung himself back under the bed. **No turn me in! No send me back! Free at last! Free at last!**

Logan hesitated. He could imagine all kinds of terrible places where griffins might be kept in captivity, studied like lab rats or trapped like dangerous wild animals. Then again, Zoe and Blue didn't exactly seem like evil government scientists.

Google said "snappa" was a drinking game. He guessed that wasn't what Zoe was talking about. Logan tried typing "snapa" instead.

"The School Nutrition Association of Pennsylvania," he muttered, frowning at the screen. "Somehow I don't think that's it, either."

So Googling wasn't going to help him. He looked down at Squorp again. The griffin cub was flopped out with his front paws over his beak, making what he probably thought were despairing noises.

"Is it so bad where you came from?" Logan asked.

Oh, terrible! Never enough to eat! All stuffed in one cave! Bossed around day and night! No treasure anywhere! Dragons staring at us all the time!

Logan clutched his head. *"Dragons?"* He had to sit down on the floor. Griffins were one thing. If there were dragons in this one-horse town, too, he had really got Xanadu all wrong.

Squorp poked his head out and tilted it at Logan. **Worst of all . . . never enough to EAT!**

"Okay, okay," Logan said. "I get the message. I'll get you some food." He hesitated. Were griffins allowed to eat hamburger? What if he accidentally poisoned Squorp?

Logan turned back to his computer and Googled "what do griffins eat?"

"Humans!" one site offered cheerfully. Logan raised an eyebrow at Squorp. The cub didn't seem like the man-eating type.

A few other websites suggested horse meat or oxen. So, at least they were carnivorous. Hamburger meat couldn't be too bad for them.

And treasure? Squorp chirped. **Need treasure! Would be best day ever!**

"Sorry, I don't have any treasure, Squorp."

Oh, no? What about this? The griffin wriggled out from under the bed, dragging a shoe box with him.

Logan reached for it. "That's nothing." But the griffin cub batted his hand away and lifted off the lid as though it were the undisturbed tomb of an Egyptian pharaoh. He plucked out several postcards of wild jungles and vast desert landscapes.

See? Treasure! Pretty! Traveled long distances to get here, yes? And carefully kept.

"They're really not important." Logan shoved himself to his feet. "Just put them back, okay?" Squorp reluctantly dropped the postcards into the box. "Come on, I'll fix you some food." He heard scrabbling in the shoe box behind him as he headed for the door.

But THIS is treasure! Squorp bounded past him

and raced to the kitchen, brandishing a shiny gold object. His paws slipped on the smooth tiles, and his legs flew out from under him, sending the cub shooting across the floor to land with a thump against the cabinets.

Logan reached down to help him up and saw what Squorp held.

He slowly took the bracelet from the griffin. It was his mom's favorite piece of jewelry, a thin gold-link chain with little charms dangling off it—an elephant, a bird, an anteater, a fox, a lizard, and seven other animals. She came back from each trip with a new charm but never took the bracelet with her in case she lost it. Logan had this weird superstition that if she ever did come back, it would be because the bracelet was here waiting for her.

"Yeah. I guess this is treasure-like, but I can't give it to you, Squorp. I'm sorry." Logan pocketed the bracelet, trying not to think about his mom.

Squorp's wings drooped, but he perked up right away when Logan pulled the hamburger meat out of the freezer.

COW? Squorp gurgled. All for ME? ALLLLLLL THIS COW??

"Uh, sure," Logan said, sticking the meat in the micro-wave. He'd have to tell his dad he'd had a serious hamburger craving. He wondered for a brief second what his father would think of Squorp, and if he might even let Logan keep him.

But that fantasy slammed into the memory of all the

conversations they'd had about how much work a dog would be. He could just imagine how this one would go. "But Dad, it'll be way easier than a schnauzer! It's probably only going to be nine times the size of a Newfoundland! And who wouldn't want a telepathic pet with claws and wings?"

Not that it was an option anyway. He had to give Squorp back to Zoe.

Besides, Logan's dad worked for the Wyoming wildlife department. They watched out for endangered species and stuff like that. Logan was pretty sure he would want to report a real, live griffin to his boss, which sounded like the worst-case scenario for Zoe and Blue, and probably Squorp as well.

While he was thinking, the griffin managed to hop up on to the green-tiled kitchen counter by bouncing several times on his talons and flapping his wings like mad, knocking over everything within reach. Logan rescued the salt shaker from under the kitchen island and replaced the spatulas in the utensil holder, trying not to laugh.

Squorp poked the fridge with his beak. **Doesn't smell like food,** he complained. **Or else Squorp would have checked in there. So hungry! All day! All alone with small scritchies taunting me!** He gave Logan a reproachful look.

"I highly doubt Mr. and Mrs. Smith were taunting you," Logan said. "And I'm glad you didn't find the fridge, because I have no idea how I'd explain to Dad why I'd eaten everything in the house."

Ahh, Squorp warbled in a tone of ancient wisdom. **Squorp know all about dads.**

"Tell me more about where you come from," Logan said, piling squashy, dripping meat on a paper plate in front of Squorp. "What do Zoe and Blue have to do with it?"

Worry-Cub and Fish-Boy? They feed us. Squorp sucked up a huge mouthful of hamburger and flapped his wings with glee. **Not very well! Not like this!**

Logan felt a surge of worry. What if griffins could only handle a small amount of food before exploding? What if you weren't supposed to feed them between noon and midnight or else they'd try to eat people? He didn't really know *anything* about griffins; and since they weren't even supposed to *exist*, anything he'd found online could be completely wrong.

"So you escaped because you were hungry?" he asked. The hamburger meat was disappearing fast.

And to find treasure! The websites Logan had scanned all said griffins were fierce protectors of their gold. It was funny to think of the little cub fiercely protecting anything, though.

Squorp opened his beak wide, paused for a long moment, and then went "SQUOOOOOOOOOOOOOOOORP." A blast of meaty breath hit Logan in the face, and he waved his hand in the air.

"Nice, Squorp," he said. "Very civilized."

The griffin clacked his beak, looking pleased with himself.

"Listen," Logan said. "I'd love to keep you, but I think you probably need to go home."

NOOO! Squorp wailed. He flopped over on the counter and covered his head with his wings. *No home! Home terrible! Terrible terrible! Everyone bossing me around! Keeping food from me! Making me go to bed when NOT EVEN TIRED!*

"That does sound terrible," Logan said. "Maybe . . . maybe you should take me there."

Squorp stopped writhing and gave Logan a sharp-eyed look. *Take you there?*

"Sure." Logan tried to look casual, like he wasn't really dying of curiosity. How did Zoe and Blue keep this secret? And what else might be hidden away with the griffins and dragons? "You can show me how terrible it is."

Squorp bounced back onto all fours and waved his tail like a cat.

Squorp show Logan all the dreadfulness! And the no food! And the dragons! And the tiny cave! And the NO FOOD!

"Yeah, okay. Sounds like a plan," Logan said, grinning at Squorp.

The griffin's long, curved beak did something very much like a smile.

Squorp show Logan the Menagerie.

FIVE

*W*here could they be?

    Zoe turned to look back at the empty street.

They must be in town somewhere. But where are they all hiding?

She and Blue had been all over Xanadu, and while they'd found lots of feathers, they hadn't spotted a single griffin cub.

Or maybe Dad's right and they're all out in the wilderness by now.

But she knew these cubs. She was sure they'd stay close to town—close to people, to familiar food, to all the interesting new smells they'd find outside the Menagerie.

There was a sharp pain at the base of her neck, as if she'd been tensing her shoulders for too long. She tried rolling her head from side to side as they waited for the light to change.

Her life was always crazy, but searching for missing griffin cubs was a whole new level of stressful . . . especially when everyone thought their escape was her fault.

Across the street, something drifted along the library steps.

"Blue!" she cried, reaching over to grab his arm. "Look!"

"Definitely a feather," he said. It was dark gray-blue—the color of one of the female griffin cubs.

"She's the one who likes books!" Zoe said. "She curls up in my lap and lets me read to her. Not a big fan of *The Crucible*, though. That one she tried to eat a couple of times."

"Really?" Blue said. "I kind of liked it."

"Me, too," Zoe said absently, her mind on the griffin. "Come on, let's check inside."

They locked their bikes in the bike rack, and Zoe hurried into the library ahead of Blue. The librarians at the desk were calmly stamping books. She could see three little kids playing with the alphabet puzzles in the children's room. An old couple peered at one of the computer catalogs together, wearing matching confused frowns.

"Looks like good news," Blue said, coming up behind her. "Nobody's screaming or running around in a panic."

"Yay," Zoe said.

"Or taking photos and uploading them instantly to the internet," Blue added.

"Okay, wow. I didn't think I could be more anxious, but now I am," said Zoe. "Thanks for that."

"Want to head upstairs?" he suggested. "No one ever goes into the back corners of the nonfiction section. Maybe she's hiding there."

"She doesn't like nonfiction," Zoe said. "She jabbed her beak right through my history book. And I'm pretty sure Mrs. Novik didn't buy my story about a bald eagle trying to steal it." She sighed. "But okay, let's check."

Another feather was lying on the second step of the stairs, so the griffin had definitely come inside. Zoe was about to swoop it up when she heard someone purr "Hey, Blue" from behind her.

She knew that voice way too well. Zoe grabbed the feather and hid it behind her back as she turned around.

Jasmin Sterling stood in the doorway of the teen room with a stack of three books propped on her hip. Her short-sleeved white angora sweater glowed against her skin, and her long, dark hair brushed the top of her skinny jeans.

As usual, she wouldn't even look at Zoe.

"Hey, Jasmin," Blue answered. "Whatcha reading?"

"*The Hunger Games*," she said, glancing at her books. "Jonathan said I'd like it."

Zoe loved *The Hunger Games*. Six months ago, she and Jasmin would have read it together and then stayed up all night talking about the movie and arguing about who was cuter, Peeta or Gale. But when you couldn't be friends with someone anymore and it was your own fault, you didn't get to be sad about all the things you'd never do together now.

The stairs trembled under Zoe's sneakers. She backed up against the wall as Jasmin's dad came jogging down, his smile big and toothy like it was in all the ads about him running for mayor. Had he seen the feather behind her back?

He stopped on the step above her. "Zoe Kahn," he said, doing a little finger gun at her. At least he didn't say "We haven't seen you around lately!" anymore like he had for the first three months.

"How's your sister?" he asked instead, which was nearly as awkward. "Enjoying college?" He didn't wait for an answer. "Jonathan loves it. We can barely get him on the phone between crew practice and a cappella rehearsals. Luckily he runs out of clean laundry every few weeks, so he's home for the weekend."

Zoe never knew what to say to Jasmin's parents, so she stuck with her usual response. "That's great, Mr. Sterling."

"Dad," Jasmin said. "You're being boring."

"Hello, Blue. Good to see you, too." Mr. Sterling looked Blue up and down as though Blue were a new wind energy factory he was thinking of buying. Mr. Sterling owned half the land surrounding Xanadu. He would have owned more if Zoe's grandparents hadn't long ago bought up the acres around the Menagerie.

She wondered if he knew about Jasmin's crush and if that was why he always looked at Blue funny. Well, he didn't have to worry. After the Ruby-Jonathan disaster, Zoe and Blue were forbidden to date anyone.

"Going upstairs?" Mr. Sterling asked. "You two can share our table." He beckoned to Jasmin, who rolled her eyes at Blue like *Aren't parents sooooo embarrassing?*

"Uh—no thanks," Zoe said. They couldn't prowl around upstairs with Jasmin and her dad watching their every move. And if they found the griffin, then what? Drag it yowling out of the library in front of everyone?

They needed a better plan. And a Sterling-free zone.

"You sure?" said Mr. Sterling. "I just found the weirdest feather up there. I've got a book on wild birds in Wyoming, and I'm going to try to figure out which one it comes from."

"*DAD,*" Jasmin said. "Total YAWN already."

Zoe hoped she didn't look as queasy as she felt. Her phone buzzed. Grateful for the distraction, she crouched down, snuck the feather inside her backpack, and rummaged through it until she found the phone, a hand-me-down from Ruby when she got an iPhone for college.

The text said **Stop panicking**.

Zoe took a deep breath and glanced at Blue, who had already tucked his phone away again. His face was all inno-cence as he listened to Jasmin's story about how Marco Jimenez had eaten corn he'd brought from home for lunch today and wasn't that so weird because who didn't like pizza?

There was also a text Zoe had missed from her brother. **Get home quick**, it said. **Apparently I have no idea how to feed a phoenix with the proper respect.**

Zoe deleted the text as fast as she could, frowning. Matthew was never careful enough about that stuff. What if someone stole her phone, or his? She'd have to delete the outgoing message from his phone later, too, since he would never do it even if she reminded him a million times.

"We gotta go, Blue," she said. "But thanks, Mr. Sterling."

"Good luck with the bird ID," Blue said. Zoe wished she could ever be that casual. He nudged Jasmin. "Let me know how the book is."

"I will," she said, smiling as if he'd asked her to prom.

"Make sure your parents vote in November!" Mr. Sterling beamed at them. "Hey, I think I've got some campaign buttons in here." He reached into his jacket pockets.

"DAAAAAAD. Wouldn't it be easier to just *shoot me* instead of *embarrassing* me to death?" Jasmin shoved her dad up the stairs ahead of her and fluttered her fingers in a goodbye wave to Blue.

Poor Jasmin, Zoe thought as she followed Blue out the door. She knew how long Jasmin had liked Blue. But Blue was exactly that nice to every girl in school, and as far as Zoe knew he didn't like any of them as more than friends.

She stopped by her bike, biting her thumbnail. "Should

we go back in?" she asked Blue. "I don't want them to see us looking for the cub, but what if they find her themselves? Or what if she escapes before we get back?"

"Then we'll deal with it," Blue said. "Try to bring your freaking out down to an eight. I don't need my best friend going gray before she's fourteen." He punched her shoulder and bent to unlock his bike.

Zoe glanced up and saw Jasmin and Mr. Sterling watching them from an upstairs window. They might be thinking about birds and Blue right now, but if they knew what was in the library with them . . . if anyone ever found out . . .

Her headache was back, worse than ever.

Please, if anyone out there is listening, she prayed, *please please help us get those cubs back.*

SIX

Logan expected Zoe's house to be big when he realized it was on the far side of town, but he was still shocked by its size as he biked up to it. He'd only seen one bigger house anywhere in Xanadu, and that was the Sterling mansion, surrounded by STERLING FOR MAYOR signs, five blocks away. Logan had biked past it a few times, wondering what it would be like to be that rich.

But somehow he'd never noticed Zoe's rambling gray stone house, or the giant matching wall that abutted it. Both were hidden from the street by a thick copse of trees. It was only when Logan turned up the crooked driveway that he could see the wall stretching for what looked like a mile in each direction away from the house.

Squorp had barely squeezed into Logan's backpack for the ride over, although he kept scaring the daylights out of Logan by popping his head out to see the view. Logan could just imagine explaining to a police officer that no, that wasn't an endangered bald eagle in his bag—just a mythical griffin, nothing to see here, carry on.

He got off his bike and wheeled it into the trees, out of sight of the driveway. Squorp wriggled his beak through the zipper again, and Logan swung the bag off his back to let the griffin out.

"Should we go up and ring the doorbell?" Logan asked.

No no no! Squorp tumbled to the ground, landing in an ungraceful heap. Logan had to hide his smile.

With a *harrumph* sound, Squorp shook the dust off his wings. **Main house is where Worry-Cub and Danger-Smell and Treasure-Paws and rest of family live. Squorp take you to dismal cave now.**

Close up, the wall around the property was even taller than Logan had thought. *Somebody clearly doesn't want their neighbors in their business.* He glanced at Squorp. *I guess I know why.*

"Squorp, how are we getting inside?" Logan stepped back and peered upward. "Even if you can fly over this wall, I can't."

Too young for flying. SUPPOSEDLY. Around,

around. Squorp take you to super-stealth entrance. The griffin fluffed up his chest and bounded off.

After fifteen minutes of walking, scrambling over fallen trees, and being clawed by bushes, Logan still couldn't spot any gaps or gates. He was getting worried. Not to mention impressed with how much land the Kahns owned.

Enough for lots of griffins and dragons, he thought. He was trying not to get too excited. Maybe Squorp was exaggerating about the dragons.

"Squorp, how much farther is the super-stealth entrance? Not that this is starting to feel like a wild-goose chase or anything."

Ha! Goose chasing not this fun, no fun at all! Tried it once. Very bad game. Our goose no good at being chased. Very pokey-snappy with beak. Squorp tail sad for DAYS.

Squorp crashed ahead through a thicket of yellow leaves and brambles. Logan decided to go around. Five minutes later Squorp came to a stop in front of a stretch of wall that looked just like the rest.

But as Logan approached, he saw a small creek running under the wall. Somebody had sliced through the grate that covered the opening and bent back the wires to create a hole Logan or a griffin cub could easily fit through.

Squorp turned around and clacked his beak at Logan. **See? No fly. Swim!**

"That's how you got out?" Logan asked. He peered at the grate. "Griffin claws can do that?"

Don't think so. Squorp gave his claws a curious look, as if he expected them to explain their abilities. **Not sure. We found it like that.** The griffin slid down the bank of the creek, landing with a splash and a startled "Grawp!"

Cold! Bah! Forgot how cold! Quick, through hole. Logan see all the dreadfulness and then take Squorp away. Pitiful food. Lack of treasure. Terrible, terrible.

Logan paused. He didn't love swimming. And he hadn't planned on getting wet. But that would be a really, really lame excuse for missing out on dragons.

He edged down the side of the ditch, keeping one hand on the wall to steady his footing. The cold water sent a shiver rocketing up his spine. He gritted his teeth and plunged in. It was much deeper than he'd expected; his feet couldn't reach the bottom. He swam against the current up to the grate and hauled himself through the gap after Squorp.

Logan not a water creature? The griffin grinned in the almost-darkness and clacked his beak at Logan.

"Not remotely," Logan said. "Please tell me we don't have to swim far."

Not far. This way!

Logan paddled behind the griffin into a dark tunnel. Using the wall as a support, he followed the sounds of

Squorp splashing to the left. It felt like they were moving along the length of the wall instead of straight through it.

"Wow," Logan breathed. "It's pitch-dark in here."

Not to Squorp. Watch out for pipe!

Logan reached forward and felt a metal pipe running along the roof of the tunnel. "Thanks."

Up ahead he saw light coming in from the right and Squorp's silhouette waiting for him. As they emerged into the sunshine, Logan realized the water flowed through a man-made ditch. Cement walls rose up on either side, so high it reminded Logan of the moats used to keep animals within their enclosures at zoos. A few yards from the main wall the water split, curving gently to the right and left.

This way! This way!

Squorp dove down the right-hand fork and Logan followed. Up ahead the stream ended at a wide lake, but before they reached it, part of the bank dipped lower to the water, with a tree growing out of the edge. Squorp was already clawing his way up the roots. Logan quickly hoisted himself out of the water next to Squorp, wrung out the bottom of his shirt, and looked around.

They were standing in a field of overgrown grass dotted with bright yellow flowers next to a fenced-in enclosure. The fence was more than twice Squorp's height and built from planks of pale-golden pinewood, with trails of morning glory vines winding around the top. Logan was just tall enough to see over it to the scattered piles of boulders inside. Most of the boulders were flat and large enough for a full-grown lion to lie across. Tiny sparkles in the gray rocks caught the sunlight.

On the far side of the enclosure was a cave surrounded by pear trees. Logan squinted at it. Something was moving in the shadows of the cave.

"What's back there?" Logan asked.

DOWN! Squorp seized Logan's wet pants in his claws and yanked so hard that Logan tumbled right over into the grass.

"What are we hiding from?" Logan whispered, getting up into a crouch. "Is there a dragon in there?"

Worse, Squorp declared glumly. **Parents.**

SEVEN

"You mean—*your* parents?" Logan asked. "This is where you live?"

Squorp sighed heavily, his wings quivering. **Moved in a week ago. Terrible, yes?**

Actually, it looked pretty nice to Logan from what he'd been able to see. There was lots of space inside the enclosure, and everything seemed clean and sunny. He edged closer to the fence and peeked over the top again.

He stifled a gasp. A large black griffin—far bigger than Squorp—stalked out of the cave, lashing its tail. As Logan watched, the griffin strode over to one of the boulders, and Logan spotted another enormous griffin basking sleepily in the sun. The second griffin had white fur with hints of gold in its feathers.

Squorp yanked Logan down to the grass again. **What you see?**

"Two big griffins—I guess that's your mom and dad," Logan whispered.

Bossy-looking, right? Always fluttering over us.

"Well," Logan said. "I mean, that's how all parents are, right? It's not so bad to be . . . fluttered over. At least they want to be with you."

Squorp scraped his claws through the dirt. **But they have to be with Squorp. That what parents are for.**

"Yeah, well, not all parents feel that way," Logan said. "Some of them have more important things to do."

The tiny griffin looked outraged. **More important than SQUORP?**

"I'm not saying they're right," Logan said. "I'm just saying, maybe your parents aren't so bad."

Should still give us treasure of our own. And teach Squorp to fly! Not too young! Terrible! He snorted and clawed up the grass under his paws.

Logan figured it was time to change the subject. "So where are these awful dragons who won't share their treasure?"

Oh, yes. Behind you.

Logan jumped and spun around, but there were no dragons in sight. He stared across the moat. On the far side, the grass was thinner and marked with scorched patches. There were more rocks and boulders, and the stony terrain grew steeper leading up to a sheer rock wall in the distance, pitted with a few caves of different sizes. He didn't see any scales or smoke, though. Maybe the dragons slept during the day. Logan turned back to Squorp as the griffin cocked his head up at him.

We go around to smallest dragon, Squorp suggested. **Closest dragon very, very grumpy.**

Logan shivered. He wanted to see dragons, but perhaps not very, very grumpy ones.

Squorp headed away from the griffin enclosure, following the moat. Ahead of them, a paved road circled the lake and branched off toward the house. On the far side of the water stood a large white dome with a roof of wire mesh stretched across steel octagons.

"What's in there?" Logan asked, nodding at the dome.

Birds. Noisy, squawking birds. Not for eating. Nobody lets Squorp eat any of the good stuff.

"HONK! HONK! HONK!"

Shrill bellows erupted from the domed building. Squorp clacked his beak at Logan.

See? That goose. Always squawking.

Suddenly they both heard a mechanical rumble up ahead.

Quick! Squorp cried. **Into the bush. Go! Go!**

Squorp and Logan dove under a hedge. Logan peeked out

and saw a golf cart trundling around the bend of the lake, carrying two adults. The woman's blond hair was pulled into a bun, and she wore a gray pinstriped suit. The guy driving had wild dark curly hair and a beard and looked like Logan's image of a zookeeper, with a grungy, long-sleeved brown shirt and torn jeans. The worried expression on his face reminded Logan a lot of Zoe.

"I know, but it doesn't make sense," the bearded man said as the cart drew closer. "It's not like Zoe to make a mistake like that."

"Check the fence again if you like," the blond woman said. "But someone left that gate unlocked, and your daughter was the last one in there."

"She must be working too hard," said Zoe's dad.

"We're *all* working too hard," said the woman. Her voice was clipped and polished, just like the perfect small pearls in her ears and on her rings. "Except for Cobalt, obviously. If you'd let me commandeer some of his people—"

"You know we can't, Melissa. He would never allow it." Mr. Kahn sighed. "They have enough to do with the kraken, the zaratan, and the kelpie. Besides, as Cobalt keeps reminding me, per their arrangement with SNAPA, they're really more like 'honored guests' than employees."

"Ha," Melissa snorted. "He always wanted to be treated like an 'honored guest' when I was married to him, too, but I—"

The rest of what she said was lost as the golf cart moved out of range.

Poor Zoe, Logan thought. He knew how terrible he'd feel if *he'd* messed up like that.

He turned to Squorp. "All right, what's SNAPA?"

Fussy snoopers. Woke us all up to look in nooks and crannies of new den for no reason. Made humans very nervous.

"INTRUDER! INTRUDER! **INTRUDER! INTRUDER!**"

Logan clapped his hands over his ears. The voice bellowing in the air was as loud as fifty car alarms set off by a thunderstorm—so loud he didn't register what it was saying at first.

"What is that?" he yelled at Squorp.

Oh, no! Squorp flapped his wings in a panic. **Alert system! Guardians of the Menagerie! They smell intruder!**

"Someone's breaking in?" Logan glanced over at the moat.

Someone ALREADY broke in! YOU!

"INTRUDER! INTRUDER! INTRUDER!"

Logan's heart started whacking around in his chest. "We're so busted!" he cried. "Squorp, what do we do?"

Quick! Squorp nudged him in the direction of the nearest building, a ramshackle wooden structure near the lake. **RUN!**

EIGHT

Logan pelted after Squorp as the griffin charged across the road. He glanced over his shoulder and saw four dark shapes burst out of the main house. They couldn't be dogs—they were *far* too big to be dogs. Was the Menagerie guarded by wild rhinoceroses?

Squorp slammed open the door with his front claws, and they darted into the shed.

Which wasn't a shed, Logan realized as the door shut behind them. It was a stable, with three stalls for animals along each wall and a scattering of fresh hay over the wooden floor. Skylights in the roof let in small square columns of sunshine. The wood smelled newly cut, and he could see cracks of light between the boards, as if the whole building had been thrown together recently.

Safest in here. Squorp panted, flapping his wings to cool off. **Charlie and Cleo won't tell on us. Don't talk to humans much. Too superior and perfect-perfect.**

Logan glanced uneasily at the only door. If someone—or some*thing*, say something roughly the size and ferociousness of a rhinoceros—came through there, he had no way out.

Squorp trotted down the aisle, heading for a pail of bright red apples hanging outside one of the middle stalls. An embossed silver nameplate that read CLEOPATRA was nailed into the center of the door. Directly across from it hung a bronze plaque saying CHARLEMAGNE. Logan saw a brilliant white rump over each of the stall doors and felt a surge of disappointment. Charlie and Cleo were just horses.

Squorp jumped up and down, flapping furiously, until he managed to snag one of the apples with a foreclaw. He yelped with joy and sat down on the floor with it.

"Really?" Logan said. "Now seems like a good time for a snack break?" The alarm was still bellowing in the distance, barely muffled by the stable walls.

All the time good time for snacks, the griffin explained, looking unconcerned. He sank his beak into the red skin with a *crunch*.

Inside her stall, Cleopatra snorted in annoyance and swung around.

Logan gasped. On her forehead, between Cleo's dark purple eyes, was a glowing spiral horn.

Cleo and Charlie were not just horses.

They were unicorns.

Cleo leaned her head over the stall door and pointed her horn at Squorp like a dagger.

"Drop it," she growled. Logan shivered. The unicorn's voice was raspy and menacing, but it still had a weird music to it, like if wind chimes could snarl at you.

Squorp froze, then eased a step backward, gripping the apple tighter in his claws. **Cleo no like red crispy. See how she has a whole pail full!** The griffin gave Logan an imploring look.

"You could at least have asked, Squorp," Logan pointed out. "That would have been the polite thing to do."

"It *would* have been," said the unicorn haughtily. "But griffins are notoriously uncouth."

And unicorns ontoriously grumpy! She say no if Squorp ask!

"We're sorry, Miss Cleopatra," Logan said. He wondered what the proper etiquette was for asking to touch her horn. It looked like the inside of seashells. But some part of him knew she would never let him near it. "We just needed a place to, uh—stop for a moment, and . . ." He trailed off as the unicorn raised her piercing gaze to him. She sniffed sharply.

"Charlemagne?" Cleo addressed her stablemate, but her eyes pinned Logan to the floor. "I hate to bother you during your oh-so-important-yet-somehow-never-fruitful beauty rest, but do turn around. There's a new serf here who seems oddly familiar, and I can't quite place my horn on it."

"Well, no one expects a lady unicorn's brain to retain information." The other unicorn neigh-chuckled to himself as he slowly shifted around in his stall and stared at Logan. His eyes were liquid gray, like cold, early-morning sky, and he had a short tuft of hair on his chin.

Crunch crunch. Squorp had taken the opportunity to devour the apple in two bites. As Cleo huffed and swung her horn down toward him, Logan swooped to pick up the baby griffin and stepped out of range. Having Squorp's comforting warmth against his chest helped settle his nerves while Charlemagne peered at him.

"Ah." The male unicorn nodded wisely. "Of course."

"What?" said Cleopatra.

"Indeed," said Charlemagne. "It's quite obvious."

"You overgrown pony, I am going to knock this door down and come poke out your eyes if you—"

"All right!" Charlemagne snorted. "He reminds you of our adoring caretakers in the Sahara oasis menagerie. Remember how they played music for us every night?"

"That's not it!" Cleopatra stamped her hooves

impatiently. "It's not his pigmentation. Look at his eyes."

"Settle down. I'll take a closer look." Charlemagne edged forward in his stall and poked his head out toward Logan, sniffing and snorting emphatically.

Logan squirmed. He was about ready to risk the rhinoceroses just to get away from the unicorns' inspection.

"Oh ho," Charlemagne said, pulling back. "I see. It's that lanky Tracker who brought in the alicanto and the girl's smelly fur ball. That's who you're thinking of."

"Hmmm. Well, that makes no sense," Cleopatra said. She turned to Logan. "Boy, don't just stand there gawking. Do you have a purpose for being here? If not, be on your way and take that little pest with you before he steals any more of my food."

Charlemagne cocked his head. "Wait, hold your humans. I think the serf may be the cause of all the fuss out there."

Logan blanched. This was it—the unicorns were going to call out a warning, and the rhinoceroses would come charging in.

"I, uh, I didn't mean to—"

But before the unicorns could do anything, the door to the stable burst open. A slavering, enormous beast filled the frame. Squorp yowled and threw himself out of Logan's arms into the closest empty stall. Logan would have done the same, but he was too petrified to move.

It wasn't a rhinoceros after all. It was a dog . . . a dog

nearly the *size* of a rhinoceros. And although Logan considered himself a dog person, this was not the kind of dog he had in mind.

Dense black fur covered it from head to paws, and its irises burned with a scarlet glow, like the red eyes on a poorly taken photo. And right now its gaze was locked on Logan. It let out a triumphant bark, the noise low and so loud it filled the small stable and reverberated in Logan's ears.

The beast slowly paced toward Logan.

"Squorp, any chance this guy is a friend of yours?" Logan asked, backing up against the far wall.

Not allowed to play with Ripper or Killer or Jaws. Mum-mum say all bark, no bite, but to stay away.

"What is it, Ripper?" a voice called from outside the stable. "Another false alarm?"

I really hope Ripper's an ironic nickname, Logan thought as the animal stalked closer. It stopped and sat firmly in front of him, as though daring him to move. The tip of its muzzle was only inches from his throat, and a sulfuric scent wafted from its fur. Logan lowered his eyes so he wouldn't appear challenging.

"You!"

Logan looked up past the towering canine and saw Zoe Kahn standing, flabbergasted, in the doorway. Her eyes darted from the unicorns to the giant dog to the pasture outside as if she was trying to figure out where and how to hide them all before he saw them. "What—what are you doing here?"

Oh NOOOOOOOOOOO, Squorp groaned. **Soooooo busted.**

"I'm sorry," Logan said. "I didn't mean to cause trouble, but he said there were dragons, and I thought it was the best way to get him home—"

"Stop," she said, waving her hands. "Who? How did you get in here?"

Logan reached into the stall and dragged Squorp out into the open.

"Check it out," he said. "I found your dog."

NINE

Zoe stared at the new kid. He'd never even spoken to her before this morning, and now here he was, in her Menagerie. Holding a mythical creature as if he did it every day.

"I'm just kidding," he said. "I know it's a griffin."

The little golden cub batted huge, innocent eyes at Zoe. She couldn't believe it. It really was one of the griffin cubs, just sitting there in Logan's arms. Surprise and anxiety warred with relief, and relief quickly won.

"You really did! You found him!" Zoe leaped past the hellhound and scooped up the cub, expertly avoiding his sharp claws and tucking his wings neatly around him. She was so happy to have one of the griffins back that she didn't even care for the moment that a stranger had somehow snuck into the Menagerie.

"Are you okay, little guy?" Zoe cooed to the griffin as she ran her hands lightly over his feathers and fur, checking for injuries.

"He seems okay to me," said Logan. "He ate, like, a truck-load of hamburger meat at my house. Plus some mouse food. I hope that's not bad for him."

"Don't worry," Zoe said. "Griffins can pretty much eat anything." The younger ones especially were the least picky eaters in the whole Menagerie. She hugged the golden cub to her chest.

The griffin gurgled and flapped as if he wanted to be set down. He did seem fine, but Zoe had no intention of letting go of him. "Where did you find him?" she asked. "And how did you know he belonged here?"

"He was hiding in my room when I got home from school. And then he told me he lived here, with dragons, and so I asked him to bring me—"

"He *told* you? No way. Griffins can't talk to humans until they're a year old." Zoe lifted one of the cub's wings to show the thicker feathers growing in underneath. "This litter's only four months old, which is why they're scattering feathers everywhere as their new ones grow in. And look at the color of his beak—that'll get darker as he gets older. Plus he'll get bigger, although they all grow at different speeds. Not to mention I was there when he cracked his egg, so I know how old he is. Point being, he couldn't have *told* you anything. Where did you really find him?"

"I'm not lying," Logan said, sounding a bit hurt. "He was under my bed. And he does talk to me." He paused, cocking his head. "He says to tell you he has a name now, and he wants you to call him Squorp like I do."

"You can't call him Squorp!" Zoe cried, outraged. "That's the sound griffins make when they burp!"

"Mork!" Squorp declared passionately.

"Well, he likes it," Logan said. He paused again. "He says to tell you he likes it better than Leo."

Zoe sucked in a breath. She was the only one who ever called the cub that, when there was no one else around. Griffins usually announced their names after a year, once they could talk to people, but she'd been hoping Leo would pick . . . well, Leo.

"But Leo is noble and dignified," she protested. "And Squorp is so—so—"

"True?" Logan suggested. "Funny *and* true?"

She looked down at the cub, who smiled his serene eagle smile at her. "Hmmm," she said. Was it really possible? She'd never heard of griffin cubs talking to people. If they could, why didn't they talk to *her*? She was the one who read to them and fed them treats and dried their feathers for them when it rained.

"Can you believe this?" Logan said with a grin. "Can you believe we're standing here, next to a pair of unicorns, talking about what to call a baby griffin? A *griffin*, Zoe."

She tried not to smile back. A stranger in the Menagerie was serious business. Serious, SNAPA-might-shut-us-down business. She was officially not allowed to get excited about maybe having someone new to talk to.

But what was she supposed to do—not talk to him?

"This is kind of my everyday life," she said ruefully.

"Your everyday life IS AMAZING," he said.

It had been a long time since Zoe had stopped to think about the amazing-ness of the Menagerie. "Well," she said, "keep in mind it's a little less amazing when you're checking griffin cubs for ticks and trying not to get pecked." She waved one hand at the massive dog behind her. "And you do not even want to know about hellhound pooper-scooping."

"Zoe," Logan said intently, as if she needed to be woken up. He pointed at Charlie. "Unicorns! Real, live unicorns!"

Cleo snorted from her stall. "I approve of your level of awe, young man," she said. "Now if everyone could learn to bow when they enter, we'd be on the right track."

Zoe whipped around to stare at the unicorn.

"Are you finally talking to us again?" Zoe asked. She hadn't heard a word out of the unicorns in a month, but they were always having diva fits about something.

Cleo lifted her horn up in the air and stamped in a circle until her rear end was facing Zoe.

So that answered that question.

"Come on," Zoe said. "Won't you at least tell us what we did this time?"

A frigid silence answered her.

"Inform the girl," Charlie said pointedly to Logan, "that we may be speaking to *you*, as you have yet to *mortally offend* us, but we are *certainly* not speaking to *her* nor to any of the other uppity serfs around here."

"Uh," Logan said, "Charlemagne says—"

"I heard him," Zoe said. "Everyone can hear unicorns. Unfortunately."

"Oh, REALLY," said Cleo, her voice echoing against the wooden boards of her stall. "You wouldn't know it from the way we're TREATED around here."

Zoe sighed and rubbed her forehead. Mollycoddling unicorns was not on her to-do list for the day. She had enough to worry about.

They still had five griffins to locate and bring back. And then people could stop blaming her for their escape, and life could go back to normal.

"Let's go find my dad," she said. She squeezed the griffin cub against her chest. "He'll be so happy to see you, little guy."

"Gurk," the griffin protested. She would never, ever get used to calling him Squorp.

"Um," Logan said, pointing at the hellhound who still

had him fixed in her glowing red glare.

"Oh, she's not as scary as she looks," Zoe said. "Ripper, at ease." The hellhound immediately relaxed, and her enormous tongue lolled out. She even wagged her tail at Logan. Zoe didn't like the look of that. The hellhounds weren't supposed to like anyone who didn't work at the Menagerie.

Zoe fished a protein bar out of the treat bag on her hip and tossed it to Ripper. The griffin tried to snatch it out of the air, but the hellhound growled, and he shrank back into Zoe's arms.

"Protein bars?" Logan asked, watching in awe as Ripper wolfed down the snack, wrapper and all.

"Yeah," said Zoe. "My mom has this theory that if you never feed them human flesh in the first place, then they won't develop a taste for it."

Logan blinked several times. "But so they . . . they normally—"

"Most hellhounds eat people," Zoe said. "Don't you know anything about mythical creatures?"

"I know they don't exist," Logan said. He smiled at the cub. "So, no, I guess I don't know anything." He followed her past the hellhound to the door. "What is this place?"

Zoe chewed her lip, thinking. It went against all her training to tell him anything. But he'd seen way too much already. And when did she ever get to talk about the Menagerie? She had never, not once in her twelve years, gotten to tell someone the truth about her life.

"It's the Menagerie," she said slowly. It was weirdly thrilling to say it out loud. "We—my family—we've been the caretakers here for several generations. But it's really, really top secret."

"I won't tell anyone," Logan promised. It was kind of sweet that he thought they'd just take his word for it. His hand twitched toward Ripper as if he was thinking about petting her, but he wisely thought better of it. "Could I— could I maybe see a dragon before you kick me out?"

Sure thing. We give tours of our top-secret facility all the time.

On the other hand, the dragons *were* pretty cool. And Zoe had always wanted to show off the Menagerie—the one thing in her life she was actually good at, since it was the only thing she had any time for. She wondered what her parents would think of Logan. There was one thing they could do to fix this . . . but maybe they didn't have to do it right away. Maybe she could show Logan around first.

"We'll see," she said. "Come on, let's go find my dad."

TEN

That didn't go too badly, Logan thought as he followed Zoe out of the stable. She may have been surprised to see him, but at least she didn't seem like she was about to feed him to a dragon.

He pulled up short when he saw a trio of hellhounds waiting beyond the stable's door. They were drooling so much the grass below them was damp. Behind them stood a small, wiry guy who looked like he might be in high school. His hair was red-brown like Zoe's, and he had a crescent-shaped white scar next to his left eyebrow. Even though it was October, he was wearing a short-sleeved T-shirt the color of avocados, and Logan could see a web of more scars twisting down his left arm.

"Oh, wow," said the stranger. "There really is an intruder. And one of the griffins! Dude!"

One of the hellhounds growled.

"Yeah, good point, Jaws," the guy said. "He does look pretty menacing."

"Is that what he said?" Logan asked nervously.

Zoe sighed. "Hellhounds are basically just dogs. They don't talk at all. Matthew was being funny, in his cleverly not-funny way. He's my brother, but that's top secret, too."

"Why?" Logan asked. "Is he like a mythical-creature secret agent or something?"

"No, he's just annoying," Zoe said. She tossed protein bars at the three hellhounds and they all flopped to the ground, chewing. Logan noticed that one of them kept thumping his tail and giving his companions a huge, open-mouthed grin. The other hellhounds ignored him.

"I *will* be a mythical-creature secret agent one day, though," Matthew said. He lifted Squorp out of Zoe's arms. "We call them Trackers, but same basic idea. Hey, fuzz ball! Where've you been? Your dad is *freaking out.*"

Yuh-oh, Squorp groaned. **Dad ALWAYS freaking out.** His grumbling turned into a rippling series of griffin giggles in Logan's head as Matthew tickled his chin feathers.

"And who are you, exactly?" Matthew asked Logan.

"He's in my class at school," Zoe said. "He can hear the griffin cub. Did you know that was possible? He says it wants to be called Squorp, of all things. He's the only saxophone player in band and he's in the advanced readers group and the cub brought him here and the unicorns weirdly love him for some reason."

"Also my name is Logan," Logan offered.

"Oh," Matthew said with a curious expression. "I see." He unclipped a walkie-talkie from his belt and spoke into it. "Mom, tell the dragons it's okay. We found the intruder, and I think the Menagerie will survive."

The bellowing alarm finally stopped.

"Where's Dad?" Zoe asked.

"In the Aviary." Matthew pointed to the white dome. "The birds were having a tiny meltdown over the intruder alarm. They're already in a snit about all the construction going on in their space. I think Dad's trying to explain to them *again* that the updates to the heating system are for their own good."

Zoe started off through the grass toward the Aviary with Matthew and Squorp close behind. Logan edged past the hellhounds who, thankfully, stayed put.

"How many animals do you have in here?" Logan asked.

Matthew and Zoe exchanged a look before he shrugged and answered. "About thirty or so, at least of the mythical variety. Three dragons, eight griffins, two unicorns, one kraken, one kelpie, four hellhounds, a bunch of other things. Depends on if you count all the salamanders separately."

They reached the shore of the lake, where tiny waves were rippling quietly against the sand. There were a couple of small islands out in the middle of the water, one a collection of large gray boulders, the other green and round and mossy.

"Salamanders?" Logan echoed. That didn't sound very mythical or exciting.

Matthew looked amused. "The fire-eating kind, not the kind you're thinking of," he said.

"Did Mom finish putting in the extra extinguishers and safety stuff?" Zoe asked anxiously. "The SNAPA agents were really serious about that. The guy kept saying we might burn down the whole Reptile House."

"They're being hard on us because of what happened with Jonathan," Matthew said, patting her head. "Don't worry so much. We'll get it all done before Sunday."

"*And* find all the griffin cubs?" Zoe said. She rubbed her wrist absently. "I don't see how. Everything keeps going wrong. I think we're cursed."

"Maybe I can help," Logan said. "I mean—I'm not busy."

Zoe didn't answer, but she tilted her head at him as if she was seriously considering it. Logan couldn't imagine anything cooler than helping out at a mythical zoo.

"So . . . what happens to the griffin cubs when they

get bigger?" Logan asked. "I mean, do you have to find new homes for them?"

Zoe actually laughed. He hadn't thought she could do that with her face all tense the way it always was.

"Sorry," she said. "You can't have one. There are a lot of rules and a ton of training involved, plus you need the right facility and a license."

Something broke the surface of the lake beside them, and Logan jumped. It disappeared before he got a good look, but he thought it might have been a giant purplish-black tentacle.

"Uh—so, wait, how did you get a license?" he asked.

"My family got theirs a long time ago," Zoe said. "Although we have to keep renewing it these days. We're sort of descended from Kublai Khan, who had one of the first menageries ever."

"Seriously?" Logan said. "Like Genghis Khan? You're related to that guy?"

Matthew chuckled. "Him, too," he said. "You'd believe it if you ever ran into Zoe first thing in the morning."

Zoe swatted him. "Not all of us sleep like the dead. You'd be just as grumpy if Firebella's dawn song woke *you* nearly every day."

"There were plenty of zoos like this in history," Matthew said to Logan. "The Ottoman Empire had a few, the Aztecs definitely had one or two, and Louis XIV had one at Versailles. But in the 1600s, the Royal Society of Species

Preservation was formed to keep them all a secret. It's a lot safer for the animals that way. You know how many ordinary species humans have already hunted to near extinction for supposedly magical properties? Just think what they'd do if they knew about real mythical creatures."

Logan could imagine, especially if people found out about the unicorns. "How many other menageries are there now?"

"About fifty worldwide, but we're one of the largest." Zoe nodded at the lake. "And we're the only one in North America with a kraken."

Logan eyed the glassy surface of the water. "A kraken? Like the sea monster that eats ships in the Pirates of the Caribbean movies?"

Matthew snorted. "The movies never get anything right. They should hire me as a mythical-creature consultant. Wouldn't that be cool? I'd be like, 'Actually, Mr. Spielberg— oh, I can call you Steve? Cool—krakens are vegetarians. Also, unicorns have really bad attitudes. Imagine, like, mega-lomaniac llamas who can talk.'"

"Our kraken isn't *that* big," Zoe said, ignoring her brother. "And she hibernates when it's cold, which is most of the year up here."

Logan glanced at the lake again as they reached the forest-green metal door of the Aviary. That tentacle hadn't looked very asleep.

He blinked. The green island—had it been that close to

the other island before? But . . . surely it couldn't have *moved*.
He watched it for a moment while Matthew unlocked the
door, but it stayed perfectly still. Like a normal island. Hmm.

He turned back to follow the Kahns. Through the door
was a staircase down to a kind of air lock, and then another
door of twisted metal vines led into the Aviary itself. A burst
of iridescent blue butterflies scattered up in the air as the
three of them came in. Chirps and twitters of birdsong surrounded them, and flickers of bright colors darted between
the leaves.

Logan had to crane his head back to see the dome far
overhead. Giant fans whirred high in the ceiling, and a few
winged shapes were spiraling happily in the gusts they pro-
duced. It was much warmer in the dome than outside.

Zoe and Matthew were already disappearing into a tunnel of hanging vines, and Logan had to hurry to catch up.
His sneakers sounded loud on the wooden boards, and he
was pretty sure several of the birds were watching him from
behind large, heart-shaped leaves.

He spotted a tiny hummingbird zipping around Zoe's
shoulder, its chest feathers glowing pink like iridescent
raspberries.

"Whoa," he said softly to her. "What kind of mythical
bird is that? What can it do?"

"The hum of its wings can tell you the future," Zoe said
in a hushed, mysterious voice. "Listen really carefully."

Logan concentrated, but all he could hear was the stream and the hidden twitters and squawks. The hummingbird paused at a white hibiscus, ignoring Logan.

Worry-Cub making fun of you, Squorp informed him.

"Oh. Wait, was that a joke?" Logan asked.

"Yes," Zoe said, smothering her giggles. "It's just a hummingbird."

"That's not fair," Logan protested. "How am I supposed to know what's magical and what's not? Why would you have ordinary hummingbirds in here?"

"The mythical birds like having company," Matthew explained. "Most of them enjoy the noise and friendship of less-mythical birds. And a couple of them just like feeling superior to something else."

"Speaking of which," Zoe said under her breath. She lifted aside a trailing vine curtain, wound with sunset-orange flowers, to reveal a nest on a low platform.

The nest was the size of the Wheel of Fortune. Straw and curving green branches mixed with expensive-looking velvets and silks in purple and blue. Preening herself in the center was a massive white goose, as tall as Zoe, with a metallic shimmer to her orange beak. She didn't bother to look up at the visitors until her feathers were perfectly settled.

"Hi, Pelly," Zoe said. "How are you feeling today?"

Get comfortable, Squorp grumbled to Logan.

The goose sighed and stretched her long neck up before answering. In a slow, drawly, quacky voice, she said, "Oh, it is *so* sweet of you to ask. I do *appreciate* how some people seem to care about me at least a tiny bit. I would *never* want to impose on anyone, but sometimes I do think just *one* more yeti-fur blanket would make this nest at least *bearably* comfortable. It's not at all important, though. I wouldn't even mention it if I weren't sleeping so very badly. Only I might be able to produce even *more* golden eggs if I weren't so terribly exhausted, but I'm sure that's hardly important to a place as financially secure as this. Although I really am almost the only source of income you have, but of course I love my work, and I'm so *happy* to contribute. Another yeti-fur blanket is the only thing that could really make my happiness complete, but I'm sure it's too much to ask. Forget I said anything."

Logan goggled at her. A goose that laid golden eggs! He wouldn't mind having one of those in his backyard.

"No, no," Zoe said flatly. "Please. We just want you to be happy. I'll talk to Mooncrusher about getting more fur tonight, but it might take a while, okay?"

The goose sighed again, and Zoe hurriedly went on. "Anyway, we're looking for my dad. It's urgent. Have you seen him?"

"Well," the goose started slowly, but a new voice interrupted.

"*I* know where he is!" it yelped. "Why doesn't anyone

ever ask *me*? I could be so helpful if anyone cared I existed. SIGH!"

"Okay," Zoe said, putting her hands on her hips. "Nero, where's my dad?"

A gorgeous bird with fiery red and gold feathers strutted out of the trees. It was about the size of a pheasant, with dramatic trails of wispy plumage cascading in all directions. The goose stared balefully at it.

"You don't have to humor me!" the new bird declared. "I know where I'm not wanted!" A few of its tail feathers brushed the giant nest.

"You stay away from my nest," the goose hissed. "I will never forgive you for last time."

"You see?" Nero yelped. "Unloved! Unappreciated!"

"Don't be silly," Matthew said. "We all love and appreciate you."

"SILLY? Are you calling my *feelings* SILLY?" The red bird flung his wings out dramatically, and the goose snapped at him, barely missing his feathers. He sidled a few steps away from the nest without pausing his rant. "This is what I mean! No one cares about me at all! I could just DIE, and no one would even NOTICE."

"Nero, stop!" Zoe shouted.

Too late, Squorp cried.

The beautiful red bird burst into flames.

ELEVEN

"NO!" Logan yelled. He leaped forward, yanked off his hooded jacket, and threw it over the fire. Flames burst right through the fabric, taller than him, and he staggered back in the face of the blazing heat.

"What do we do?" he shouted to Zoe. She looked too astonished to react. A large palm frond was lying beside the nest, and Logan snatched it up and began beating at the fire. They'd had a fire scare at his apartment in Chicago once, soon after Mom left, when something got stuck in the toaster and small flames started shooting out the top. But this time there wasn't a fire extinguisher under a nearby sink.

And then, all at once, the fire collapsed and went out. The only thing left was a pile of charred black ashes as high as Logan's knee.

"Oh, no," Logan said. He crouched beside the ashes, feeling sick. The palm frond slipped out of his fingers. "That beautiful bird."

"We should videotape this," Matthew said to Zoe. "Nero hasn't gotten a reaction like that in about six hundred years. It would totally make his century."

"Nasty, horrible creature," Pelly the goose spat from her nest. "Did you see that? He *deliberately* tried to set my nest on fire."

"I can't believe you did that," Zoe said, her thin hands fluttering toward Logan. "I mean—your jacket . . ."

"It's not important," Logan said. He could feel heat coming off the ashes, with curls of smoke that smelled like vanilla and dates. "I can't believe we just watched something amazing die. Are they terribly endangered?"

"Well, in a way. Nero's the only one in the world." Zoe's dad stepped through another vine curtain on the far side of the nest. "But he's all right, young man. He's a phoenix. He'll be back."

Logan blinked as Mr. Kahn crouched beside him and stirred the ashes with a stick. "See?" Zoe's dad said. "There's an egg in here." A shimmering golden-white eggshell glinted through the black ashes. "Nero will be reborn from that in about . . ." Mr. Kahn checked his watch. "Half an hour."

"So if you could hang out beside the egg until then, sobbing with despair, it'd be really great for his self-esteem," Matthew suggested.

"I'm not sobbing with despair," Logan said crossly. He thought someone might have mentioned this was a magical regenerating bird before he'd burned up his jacket. Dad was really not going to be psyched about that.

"It used to happen only every five hundred years," Mr. Kahn explained, "but over time Nero's worked out how to speed it up. He's quite an expert at incinerating himself whenever he's upset about something."

"So, like, three or four times a day, at least," Zoe added.

Logan felt his cheeks getting warm. No wonder nobody else had reacted. "Sorry," he mumbled.

"Well, you didn't know," Zoe's dad said, helping him to his feet. "But it was brave of you to try to help. So . . . who are you?"

Zoe and Matthew both started talking at once, and Squorp took the opportunity to wriggle out of Matthew's arms and bound over to Logan. The warm griffin wings brushing his hands made Logan feel less self-conscious. He picked up Squorp and scratched under his chin the way Matthew had.

"Mork," Squorp gurgled, nestling into Logan's chest. His beak poked around Logan's collar, and Logan felt a tug. He looked down in time to see one of his shirt buttons disappearing into the griffin cub's mouth.

"Hey, quit that," Logan said. "I need all the clothes I have left."

"It's really not my fault, Dad, I swear," Zoe was saying. "I promise I didn't tell him anything at school, and I definitely didn't let him into the house. I don't know how he got in. I've barely ever spoken to him."

"These things happen," Mr. Kahn said. "He's not the first townie to accidentally get in here. We'll deal with it the usual way. But then, I must say I've never heard of anyone talking to griffins at this age before." He scratched his beard, looking at Logan as though he were able to whistle underwater. "What did you say your name was?"

"Logan Wilde."

"I see. And what do your parents do?"

"Nothing important." Logan didn't want to admit that his dad was with the wildlife department in case that scared the Kahns. "It's just me and my dad now."

Zoe's dad shook his head, watching Squorp. "Most unusual, your connection with the griffin. What's he saying now?"

Logan glanced down at Squorp. "He's kind of mumbling about delicious buttons. Don't even think about it, cub."

"Hey, little fellow," Mr. Kahn said. He bent down to meet Squorp's eyes. "What were you doing outside the walls?"

Much delicious food outside walls! But not much treasure. Thought there'd be more. Clink PROMISED us treasure.

At Logan's smile, Mr. Kahn looked up. "What did he say?"

"He said he liked the food, but there wasn't as much treasure as he'd thought there would be. He also says someone named Clink promised him treasure."

"Interesting. Who's Clink, buddy?"

Big furry bossy furry BOSSY. Escape her idea! And THEN outside, Clink all Okay BYE and leaves us! Probably found all the treasure and keeping it for herself. Bossy bossy.

Logan relayed this to the Kahns, more or less. Zoe snapped her fingers. "The big black griffin cub," she said. "I bet that's who he means. She always pushes the others around and decides who eats when and what they're going to play."

Bossy BOSSY, Squorp grumbled.

"So they're out looking for treasure," Mr. Kahn said. "That is useful to know." He frowned. "Maybe you're right, Zoe—maybe they're all in town, not out in the wild where we've been looking."

"I think so, Dad," she said. "I mean, we saw at least four different kinds of feathers between school and the library and the post office."

Her dad sighed. "That makes things a lot harder. Well, let's get you back to your parents, at least," he said to Squorp.

N°°, Squorp wailed, burying his head in Logan's neck. His beak jabbed uncomfortably into Logan's collarbone, but Logan didn't mind.

"It'll be all right," he said, stroking Squorp's golden fur. "Maybe I can come back and visit sometimes. I can even bring you hamburger meat, if they let me."

He looked up and caught Matthew shaking his head at Zoe. That didn't look promising. But now that he knew about the Menagerie, would they really keep him away from it forever?

Cow for me, Squorp gurgled wistfully. He draped his wings over Logan's shoulders.

Mr. Kahn carefully arranged palm fronds around the phoenix ashes. "Pelly, when Nero emerges, please tell him we hope he's all right and we'll come back to check on him later."

The goose was indignantly huddled on the far side of the nest from the ash pile. "Oh," she said, "I *suppose* it makes sense that I should also start delivering messages for everyone, since I'm already the *only* reason this menagerie can survive. It does seem *logical* that I should do even *more* work around here. Especially when it involves talking to *serial arsonists.* Don't worry about *my* feathers or *my* beautiful nest at all. No, no, I'll just sit here in the thick toxic

clouds of smoke until he crawls out and fails to apologize."
She coughed dramatically.

Logan looked down at the tiny wisp of smoke curling up
from the ashes. Zoe shook her head at him, like, *Don't bother
saying anything.*

Squorp clung to Logan as they followed Mr. Kahn out
of the Aviary and back around the lake toward the griffin
enclosure. The sun was drifting low in the sky, turning the
high trails of clouds cherry and tangerine.

Another golf cart came zipping down the path from the
house. Strapped to the back was a crate of gardening tools:
long shears, a rake, trowels, some empty pots. In the front,
driving, was an abominable snowman.

Logan pushed Squorp's feathers out of his face and
stared as the cart came closer. The driver was at least eleven
feet tall and covered in shaggy white fur, stained with dirt
and grassy green smudges, particularly around the knees
and paws. He wore a pair of enormous dark sunglasses and a
safari-type sun hat on his head. His mouth was a wide gap in
his furry face, like a Muppet's.

"Hello there, Mooncrusher!" Mr. Kahn called. "How are
the rosebushes?"

"BLAAAARGH!" answered the creature. The golf cart
reached the road around the lake and turned to drive away
from them.

"Did you see the hole by the cellar door? I think Jaws has

been trying to bury protein bars again. We need to get that filled before SNAPA returns."

"BLAAAAARRRGH!" The cart followed the curve of the lake, getting smaller.

"And don't forget the Captain's exercise!" Zoe shouted. "His ball is in your yurt!"

"BLAAAAAARGH!" A massive white paw emerged from the cart and waved. Then the cart bumped off onto another fork in the path and sped into the distance.

Mr. Kahn saw Logan's expression and smiled. "Our groundskeeper is, let's say, a yeti of few words," he said.

"Unlike all those super-chatty yetis," Matthew joked. At least, Logan guessed he was joking. "I'll go feed the hellhounds and catch up to you guys later." He whistled for the four hellhounds, who were still flopped on the ground outside the unicorn stable. They lumbered to their feet and raced him up to the house.

The door to the griffin enclosure was a solid black metal gate with unicorns facing each other on the two sides, outlined in gold. Three deadbolts punctuated the center gap like menacing buttons. Logan noticed that Zoe watched her father intently as he opened the gate, and Mr. Kahn gave her a quick, worried look at the same time.

The doors opened inward a few feet from the large, flat boulder where the white griffin was sprawled, sunning herself in the last rays of daylight. She opened one eye to a slit and peered at Squorp.

Oh, Logan heard her say. **Fantastic.**

SON! The black griffin came galloping across the rocks, flapping his wings wildly like flags in a hurricane. **You're ALIIIIIIIVE!** He braked in front of Logan and snatched the cub out of Logan's arms, crushing Squorp fiercely against his black chest.

"Mmmmmrrrk," the muffled cub objected, squirming. **Hi, Dad.**

Logan felt as if a runaway train had just careened by an inch from his face. He shoved his hands into his pockets to stop them from shaking. The black griffin's claws were as long and sharp as hunting knives, and he towered over Mr. Kahn by a few inches.

Was this how big Squorp would get?

NIRA! the black griffin bellowed. From the way Mr. Kahn and Zoe winced, Logan guessed everyone could hear the adult griffins in their heads. **Behold! One of our beautiful perfect cubs has returned to us! He's ALIIIIVE!**

That's not even remotely surprising, the white griffin answered. She closed her eyes and shifted her wings so the feathers underneath could get a bit more sun.

Come rejoice with us! Squorp's dad insisted.

Maybe later, said the white griffin.

HUNGRY! Squorp chirped.

That's not surprising, either, said the white griffin.

Your mother is thrilled that you're home, the black griffin said to Squorp. **She's been worried sick about you.**

Yes, said the white griffin without opening her eyes. **I'm definitely the one who's been tearing my feathers out all day.**

Logan glanced around. Large black feathers were scattered across the boulders.

"Logan, this is Riff," said Mr. Kahn, indicating Squorp's dad. "And that over there is Nira."

"She's usually a bit more . . . upright," said Zoe. She tilted her head at the sleepy white griffin. "Are you all right, Nira?"

It's all the anxiety, pronounced Riff. **It's worn her out.**

Nira didn't bother to respond.

What about the others? Riff demanded. **Where are my other precious cubs?**

"Maybe I could help look for the other griffins," Logan jumped in. He didn't want to go home to his empty house, and he really did not want to get shut out of this amazing place.

"I have some questions first," said Mr. Kahn. "Logan, could you ask the cub how they all got out?"

Beside him, Logan felt Zoe tense.

Clink found gate open, Squorp answered readily.

"He says the gate was unlocked," Logan said. "Then they

swam out through the moat—that's how he got me in here, too. There's a hole in the grate on the outside wall."

"Oh, God," Zoe said, dropping onto one of the boulders as if griffin wings had knocked her over. She buried her face in her hands. "Then it *was* my fault. But Dad, I never forget to lock the gate! I'm *sure* it was locked when I left last night."

"Let's not jump to conclusions yet. I'm more worried about the hole in the grate," her dad said kindly. "I'll have to speak to Cobalt about fixing that."

Why would you leave us? Riff bellowed at his son, wrapping his wings more tightly around the cub. His black lion tail lashed back and forth. **When we love you SO MUCH?**

What Logan could still see of Squorp was wriggling uncomfortably.

Just wanted treasure, Squorp said. **Clink promised treasure! Griffins supposed to have treasure!**

"Oh, hey!" Logan said with a start. "The bank! I saw something weird there on my way to school this morning. Like the front door had been clawed up—maybe one of the cubs figured out there was money inside and went looking for treasure."

"We'd better head over there right now," said Zoe's dad. He glanced at his watch. "I guess the dragon toothbrushes will have to wait until tomorrow."

"What about the library?" Zoe asked. She picked up a

stray branch and started snapping it into small pieces. "It closes at seven. And also—uh, should we offer Logan, you know—something to drink?"

"Me?" Logan said. "I'm okay."

"Let's put a temporary delay on that," said Mr. Kahn. Zoe looked oddly pleased at this answer. "Matthew and I and your mother will head to the bank. You get Blue and take Logan to the library. See if he can hear the griffin there. With luck we'll get two more cubs back here before dinner."

Squorp poked his head out between his dad's wings. **Dinner? Fish! Want fish! Me, fish, me!**

For heaven's sake, said Nira, opening her eyes. **I'm trying to get my first decent sleep in four months. Could you all take this noisy conversation elsewhere? Especially you two.** She clacked her beak at Riff and Squorp.

Let's go find you a fish, Riff said with dignity, carrying Squorp away. The cub twisted his neck around to look back at Logan.

Good luck finding brothers and sisters! Come back soon! Bring cow!

Mr. Kahn turned and strode out of the enclosure, leaving Logan and Zoe staring at each other.

"Did he say dragon toothbrushes?" Logan asked.

"Isn't that lame?" Zoe dropped the pieces of her branch and stood up, dusting off her hands. "The SNAPA agents said we're neglecting the dragons' 'dental hygiene.' There's no record of dragon toothbrushing anywhere in Kahn Menagerie history. They're wild animals! Plus their teeth are in great shape from all the volcanic rocks they eat. I swear the agents are just hoping we'll get our heads bitten off."

"What is SNAPA?" Logan asked, following her to the gate.

"The SuperNatural Animal Protection Agency," Zoe said. "Government, top secret, in charge of all the menageries. We had a surprise inspection visit from them last Sunday, and they gave us a giant list of things to fix before they come back *this* Sunday. So this is basically the worst possible time to be dealing with runaway griffin cubs, too."

"We'll find them," Logan said confidently. "I'll help. Don't worry."

Five missing griffin cubs in a small town like Xanadu.

How hard could that be?

TWELVE

Zoe wished Captain Fuzzbutt was out and about so she could hug him. That always made her feel better, but this was his exercise time with the yeti.

Had she really left the gate unlocked? Was this all her fault?

She glanced at Logan again. Part of her liked showing him around; it was fun to watch him quietly freak out about everything. But she knew it was dangerous for anyone to know about the Menagerie, and it made her nervous that her dad thought finding the griffins was a bigger problem.

"So where does Blue live?" Logan asked as they came out of the griffin enclosure. "You can use my cell if you need to call him." He reached for his pocket and stopped. "Oh, no, sorry, I left it back with my bike."

"I don't need a phone to call Blue," Zoe said. She pulled the whalebone whistle out of her hip bag and blew into it.

Logan winced, touching his ears. "You use a dog whistle to call Blue?"

"It's not a dog whistle," she said. "Or else you wouldn't be able to hear it." She crossed the lake circle road and paused at the edge of the water, her sneakers sinking into the sandy gravel. "And don't say anything like that where Blue's family can hear you. They will seriously drown you."

"Are you joking again?" Logan asked. He rubbed his arms nervously. "Are they, like, the Mob? Does the Mob have something to do with unicorns and griffins?" He paused. "Okay, if not, I am totally writing that movie."

Zoe noticed that his arms were covered in goose bumps. She'd forgotten he must be cold without his jacket. "They're not the Mob," she said. "Well, not *the* Mob. They're kind of *a* mob. You'll see."

A head poked out of the water suddenly a few feet away, and Logan literally fell over with surprise. It was almost funny, but Zoe had seen this particular gorgeous blond head way too often, and she knew the mean-girl brain inside it. Jasmin tried to be mean, but she could never be as bad as Sapphire. Plus Jasmin had too much self-respect to wear a bikini top that skimpy.

"We need Blue," Zoe said.

"This is his Dad Time, Zoe," Sapphire said in a patron-izing, can't-you-remember-anything voice. She wound her waist-length hair up on her head and fluttered her eyelashes at Logan.

"This is more important," Zoe said.

"Oh," said Sapphire with fake sympathy, "did you get lonely and finally notice he's your only friend? Or maybe you're feeling all useless and wretched because you're the first Kahn in Menagerie history to lose one of the mythical animals. Wait, did I say one? It's actually six, isn't it?"

Zoe couldn't speak for a minute. Sapphire always knew exactly how to punch Zoe in the heart. She could tell when-ever Zoe was missing Jasmin, or wishing she could try out for soccer, or worrying about how she'd ever live up to Matthew and Ruby.

Zoe knew for a fact that mermaids couldn't read minds, but Sapphire made her wonder.

"Just get Blue," Logan said, climbing to his feet beside her. Sapphire gave him an icy look. "Uh . . . please?"

The blond mermaid dove with a swish of her emerald tail that splashed them both.

"That was a mermaid!" Logan hissed. "A—well, kind of a mean mermaid."

"They're pretty much all like that. Except Blue."

"Blue's a—"

"*Don't* call him a mermaid," Zoe said. "Trust me, it doesn't go over well. But he doesn't like merboy, either. And merman sounds totally weird. Merguy? I just avoid calling him anything but Blue."

"So was that his sister?"

"No, no, no," Zoe said, shaking her head firmly. "Blue's an only child. She might be his second or third cousin or something—I can't really keep track of how all our merfolk are related."

"That is—" Logan trailed off as Blue came striding out of the lake. Shimmering blueberry-colored scales were still melting into the skin around his waist. Logan threw his hands over his eyes.

"Relax," Zoe said, trying not to laugh. "He puts on shorts underwater before he comes up. We have a strict no-mermaid-nakedness policy." *Which most of them hate,* she thought.

"Oh, thank God," Logan said, dropping his hands.

"Hey, Logan," Blue said casually, grinning, as if it didn't surprise him at all to find the new kid hanging out inside the Menagerie with Zoe. He took a towel from the storage chest beside the water and toweled off his hair.

Zoe saw the happy look that flashed across Logan's face. He hadn't thought Blue would know his name. That was kind of sad, actually.

"Hey, Blue," Logan said, trying to sound equally casual.

"We're going to the library," Zoe said. "I'll explain—

this—on the way." She waved her hands at Logan.

"Cool," Blue said. "Man, you look cold. Want to borrow a jacket?"

"Nah, I'm good," Logan said. He adjusted his stance to look a bit tougher. Of course, Blue was standing there, dripping wet, in nothing but shorts. Boys could be so dopey when they were trying to be macho.

"Yes, he does," Zoe said. "He lost his jacket trying to save Nero from one of his temper tantrums. But hurry up. We only have half an hour before the library closes."

Blue jogged ahead of them to the house, and when he emerged, fully dressed, he handed Logan a dark-green hooded sweatshirt.

"All right, thanks," Logan said. He put it on while Zoe and Blue wheeled their bikes out of the garage. His brown eyes went even bigger when he saw the silver fire-retardant suits hanging on the walls between the golf carts and dragon harnesses.

But his next question wasn't about dragons. As he picked up his own bike in the trees outside the wall, he said to Blue, "So, do you live in the lake?"

"Some of the time," Blue said. "That's where my dad is. The rest of the time I'm up at the house with my mom."

"Oh," Logan said. "So they're—"

"Yeah. Divorced," Blue said. "It sucks. But whatever." He shrugged.

"And now the whole colony won't shut up about what a mistake it is for merfolk to marry humans," Zoe said. Logan tilted his head curiously, and she guessed what he was thinking. "They're not talking about *us*, dorkface. Blue's like my brother. Gross. I want to strangle him, like, fifty times a day."

Besides, she would never do that to Jasmin, even if they weren't speaking anymore.

"Oh, but if it comes up at school," she said, "everyone there thinks Blue and his mom rent an apartment in our house."

It was mostly downhill to the library. Usually Zoe loved the feeling of the wind flying through her hair, but out in front of the others she had no one to distract her from her worries about the griffin gate.

Surely this couldn't be her fault. She *had* locked it. She *knew* she had.

But if that was true . . . then who had unlocked it?

THIRTEEN

Blue didn't seem quite as stunned as everyone else by Logan's ability to hear baby griffins.

"That's cool," he said. The three of them were across the street from the library. The sun was nearly all the way down, and it was quickly getting cold and dark outside. As far as Logan could tell, they were waiting for Zoe to make a plan.

"Mostly Squorp talks about food," Logan said to Blue. "It's not, like, deep conversation."

"Sounds useful, though. They get so mad when we don't understand them." He held out his arm to show Logan a bruise on his wrist. "The black one bit me a couple days ago when I gave her a fish to stop her yelling. Still not sure what she really wanted."

"Maybe treasure," Logan joked.

Blue's eyes went thoughtful. "Actually, yeah, maybe," he said.

"Can't their parents tell you what they're saying?" Logan asked.

"Nira's too busy," Blue said. "And Riff's too frantic."

"Six cubs are a lot to handle," Zoe said. "This is their first litter." Her voice glowed with pride. "The Kahn Menagerie has the best griffin-breeding record in the world. Mom and Dad raised Riff's litter and traded one of his brothers to another menagerie for Nira. We knew they'd be perfect together."

Logan remembered the sleepy, disgruntled white griffin and wondered if that was true. But he wasn't about to question the best griffin-breeding record in the world.

"So what do we do now?" he asked, nodding at the library.

"We leave our bikes by the pizza place," Zoe said. "That way the librarians won't see them when they leave. Then we'll hide in the library until it closes." She checked her watch again. "Ten minutes. Hurry."

The pizza place was only a block away. As they leaned their bikes against the alley wall, Logan noticed that the restaurant was closed, which seemed weird for a Friday night. He tried to peer in through the dark window, but he couldn't see anything. Except maybe—was that a puddle of tomato sauce on the floor?

"Come *on*." Zoe yanked on Blue's sleeve and took off toward the library.

Logan and Blue followed. Logan liked how Blue never rushed. He matched the taller boy's pace as they strolled up the stairs into the library. Zoe had already vanished inside.

"Hold up," Blue said, stopping to inspect a notice on the bulletin board. Logan looked at it, too. It was about some rancher meeting to discuss a bunch of missing sheep. He glanced at Blue. What—

"Okay, now," Blue said. Logan realized that the lone librarian at the desk had bent down to empty the book drop. They were able to go by without being seen. Logan grinned. *Slick, Blue.*

Blue took the stairs two at a time with his long legs. At the top he slowly pivoted, scanning the aisles of books, round wooden study tables, and armchairs tucked into dark corners. Logan did the same. All he saw was Zoe pacing nervously past the shelves, glancing along each one. There were a lot of walls and tall bookshelves, so it was impossible to see every part of the floor from anywhere. The few people left at the tables were packing up their bags and heading downstairs.

"The library will be closing in five minutes," said a voice over the PA system. "Please bring all materials to the front desk to check out."

"Why, hello there." The school librarian emerged from one of the stacks, carrying a pile of books. Her lime-green skirt looked a bit less startling here, away from school. She smiled at them. "How nice to see some of my students at the library on a Friday night."

"Hey, Miss Sameera," Blue said, shaking his hair out of his eyes. "Need help with those?" He reached for her books, but she took a quick step back.

"No, no," she said. "Nothing interesting here. Just a private project." She gave an odd little laugh. Logan couldn't be sure, but he thought she was deliberately holding the books so they couldn't read the titles.

Huh, he thought. *Must be something really embarrassing.*

"See you on Monday," she said brightly, and hurried off down the stairs with her skirt mirrors tinkling and flashing as she went.

Curious, Logan leaned over the stairs to watch her check out. He couldn't read the book titles from where he was, but one of them had a pair of rearing unicorns on the cover, and another one looked like it was about sea serpents.

Weird.

"Let's hide," Blue said, bringing Logan's attention back to the griffin search. "Looks like Zoe already has." He led Logan down one of the long aisles and along the back wall of windows to a pair of plain wooden doors. White letters on black labels said HEMINGWAYS on one door and BRONTËS on the other.

"I don't get it," Logan said, reading the signs.

"I didn't either at first," Blue said. "Zoe explained it. That one's Men, like Ernest Hemingway, and that one's Women, like the Brontë sisters. It's a library joke."

Logan didn't think it would be very funny if he'd accidentally walked into the girls' bathroom because he'd never heard of the Brontës.

They went through the "Hemingways" door and each hid in a stall. Logan was glad the doors went all the way to the ground so he didn't have to stand on the toilet.

"This is like that book," he whispered. "Where the kids run away and stay in the Metropolitan Museum? Remember? They hid in the bathrooms every night from the security guard. After I read it, I made my mom take me to the Art Institute so I could figure out where I'd sleep if I was spending the night there." He stopped. His mom had loved the book, too. She hadn't looked at her Blackberry once that whole day.

"When did your parents get divorced?" he asked to change the subject.

"Pretty soon after I was born," Blue's voice said over the partition. "They're not big fans of each other."

The bathroom door opened, and Logan shut his mouth quickly. He pressed his back against the wall. *Please don't check all the stalls*, he prayed.

"Anyone in here?" It sounded like one of the librarians,

who spoke with a quiet midwestern accent. The lights flashed off and on a couple of times, and then went off. They were plunged into darkness as the door closed.

Logan exhaled softly.

"Now we wait a few minutes," Blue whispered.

Logan had a million more questions about the Menagerie, but he didn't want to break the silence. So he just waited until finally he heard Blue step out of his stall and open the door.

The library looked like a whole different place in the dark. Moonlight came through the windows, turning everything purple and silver. Long shadows crawled across the rug from the shelves and furniture, like puddles of melted night creatures.

"I'll go this way," Blue said, pointing along one wall. "You go that way. We'll run into each other on the other side of the building."

"We don't have to find Zoe first?" Logan asked.

"Don't worry," Blue said. "She'll find us."

Logan started off along his wall, which was not the one with windows. The room got darker and darker as he went forward. His hands bumped into a doorknob on his right, but the door was locked. Administrative offices, maybe. He peered down each dark aisle, but it was hard to tell what was shadow and what might be griffin cub unless he walked up and down, so he started doing that, wishing he had a flashlight.

He reached the far wall, where a bank of tall windows looked out on the front of the library. Here there was bright moonlight again. The street outside was quiet. Logan glanced at the sidewalk below.

A shiver ran down his spine. Was there something . . . or some*one* . . . in the shadows of the trees?

Logan edged slowly away from the windows. He didn't think anyone could see in, but still, he had a strange, creeping feeling that someone was out there, just standing, staring toward the library.

FOURTEEN

Find the cub and get out, Logan told himself uneasily. This wasn't the right way to look. If someone could see the griffin as they walked along an aisle, she'd have been spotted hours ago. *Where would I hide in here if I were the size of a big puppy?*

Or where would I go if I were looking for treasure?

"Zoe?" he said quietly.

"Over here," she whispered. He found her behind the upstairs information desk, checking cabinets.

"Why would the griffin come here?" he asked. "What would make her think there's treasure in a library?"

"This one likes it when I read out loud," Zoe said.

"Maybe books *are* treasure to her."

"Aww," Logan said. "So she's like the teacher's pet of griffins."

"She *is* my favorite," Zoe admitted, tucking her hair behind her ears. She opened the last cabinet and sighed.

"What's her favorite book?" Logan asked. "Does she have one?"

"Of course," Zoe said. "Harry Potter, obviously."

"Makes sense," Logan said. "I'm going to check the children's room."

He hurried to the stairwell in the center of the building. On the ground floor there was an archway painted with characters like the Very Hungry Caterpillar, Olivia, and the Wild Things. He'd never actually gone through it into the kids' room before.

The windows were bigger and the shelves were lower in here, with rows of "Librarian's Picks" picture books propped up on top of them. Posters of Newbery and Caldecott winners lined the walls, and a few of the tables had wooden puzzles neatly stacked on them. A fish tank blooped quietly, glowing an eerie blue next to the circular main desk.

There was no sign of a griffin cub. At least not until Logan checked the "R" shelves and found all the J. K. Rowling books missing.

He looked around the big room again and spotted a glass door at the back. A finger-painted sign taped to the glass said: STORYTIME ROOM! A list of days and times was posted next to the door. Logan noticed that Friday was not one of the days listed.

Through the glass Logan could see a small room with a cheerful ABC mat covering the floor. Three fabric toy boxes of board books and kid instruments were lined up in one corner. In the other corner was a little wooden playhouse as tall as Logan.

He tried the knob, but the door was locked. *That means she couldn't be in there, right?*

Still . . .

Logan went back to the main desk in the middle of the room and slipped behind the counter. Pencils, bookmarks, and stickers covered its surface. . . . Then he saw something glint in the moonlight. Two keys were hanging on a hook under the desk. He lifted them up a little guiltily and headed back to the kids' room. Sure enough, one of them fit the Storytime Room door.

As he pushed it open, he heard a rustling from the playhouse.

"Griffin cub?" he whispered. "It's okay. I'm here to help you."

There was a long pause. Finally a beak and a pair of dark eyes peeked out of the playhouse window.

Really? said the griffin's voice in his head.

"I promise," Logan said. "My name is Logan. I'm here with Zoe and Blue."

The griffin threw her wings open and came tumbling

out of the back of the playhouse. She galloped up to Logan, and for a moment he was afraid she'd run right past him and escape again. But instead, with a great deal of flapping, she launched herself up and into his arms.

Her soft, dark-gray wings wrapped around his shoulders, and she buried her head in his neck.

So worried! she said. **Flurp found such beautiful treasure, such perfect treasure, and then the tall ladies came and Flurp hid, so fast! So well! With treasure in good hiding place! But then Flurp came out and DOOR LOCKED! Flurp stuck! Flurp trapped! What good treasure without FREEDOM?** She picked up her head to look at him soulfully. **Flurp learned valuable lesson today.**

"So you're ready to go home?" Logan asked.

Flurp settled her paws against his chest and tucked her tail over one of his arms. **Flurp ready to write fabulous tales of grand adventure. Flurp ready to be most famous author of all time! From nice warm safe cave with much fish.** She clacked her beak. **Nothing to eat in here but BOOKS.**

"Did you actually—?" Logan glanced through the playhouse window. The floor was covered in Harry Potter books, as if Flurp had been making a nest out of them.

Eat books?! Flurp would NEVER! Flurp would STARVE first!

The griffin cub let out a tiny burp that smelled of crayons.

"Yikes," Logan said. "Let's get you to some real food."

Zoe and Blue were coming down the stairs as he walked out of the children's room. Zoe gasped and ran up to him when she saw the griffin in Logan's arms.

"Nice work, Logan!" Blue said.

"Thanks." Logan shifted the griffin, trying not to grin too hugely.

"Are you all right?" Zoe asked the cub. She stroked the little ruff of soft feathers around the griffin's neck. "I was really worried about you."

Flurp leaned her head into Zoe's fingers and gave her a serene griffin smile. **Much better now. So HAPPY to be going back. Worry-Cub never mentioned that no food allowed in libraries!**

"She says she's better now," Logan told Zoe. "Her name is Flurp, by the way."

Zoe groaned. "Flurp?" she said to the griffin cub. "What was wrong with Hermione? I thought you'd love that!"

Logan listened for a minute. "She says Hermione is great, but Flurp is an original. No copycatting for the one and only Flurp."

With a sigh, Zoe smoothed Flurp's wings. "Well, it's better than Squorp," she said. Flurp made a sound like a chuckle.

Suddenly Blue grabbed Zoe and Logan and pushed them

into the space under the stairs. Flurp squawked indignantly, and Blue wrapped one hand around her beak, shushing them all. He pointed at the front door.

A yellow light was bobbing outside—low and small, like a flashlight.

Logan held his breath. He could feel Zoe doing the same thing beside him. Even Flurp went perfectly still, like Logan's mice whenever they spotted Purrsimmon.

The light moved closer as the dark figure behind the flashlight walked up the steps of the library. It had to be the person Logan had seen in the shadows outside. But why would someone be lurking around the library at this hour?

The flashlight beam shone through the glass windows, scanning slowly across the carpeted floor. It traveled over the circulation desk and the bulletin board, the elevator door and the display case of Halloween books and horror stories. The light passed a few yards from Logan's sneakers.

Finally the dark figure backed away, shining the light up at the second floor. After a moment, he or she went down the steps, but instead of walking away, the bobbing light began to circle around the building.

"Who is that?" Logan whispered. It seemed like his pulse was beating in his ears, it was going so fast.

"I have no idea," said Blue. "Do you think they know we're in here?"

"Or about the griffins?" Zoe said worriedly. "Blue, what

if it's an exterminator? What if SNAPA found out about the escape somehow?"

Logan pulled the griffin cub closer. "Exterminator?" he echoed. Flurp poked her beak inside his jacket, trembling.

"They're not real," Blue said. "It's an urban legend Matthew brought back from Tracker camp."

"It could be true," Zoe insisted. "Matthew said some Trackers are chosen for a different path—hunting down escaped creatures to kill them instead of capture them. Like when they're too dangerous, or when SNAPA thinks they're not worth saving."

"They wouldn't do that to the cubs," Blue said. "Even if exterminators do exist, which I don't think they do."

Zoe bit her nails, staring at the front door. Logan felt like the dark shadows were getting thicker and heavier around them. For the first time, he realized there was more to the Menagerie than hanging out with cool animals.

"How do we get out?" Logan asked.

"We run," Zoe said. "Especially you, because you have, uh, Flurp. If that guy sees us, Blue and I will distract him so you can get away." She pulled a black cloth out of her backpack; when she unrolled it, it turned out to be a kind of giant sling. Zoe reached to fit it over Logan's shoulders.

"Wait," Logan said, catching her wrist. "You should take Flurp. You have to be the one who gets away. If they catch me, I'm just a random guy who snuck into the library. But once they know who you are, they might find out about your family and the Menagerie."

Blue nodded in agreement.

"Okay." Zoe didn't argue. She took Flurp gently out of Logan's arms, and the boys lifted and wound the sling around her shoulders until the griffin cub was well hidden.

Logan peeked out from under the stairs. A hallway led from the circulation desk to the café and, in the distance, the back door. He spotted the flashlight beam sweep past the rear windows.

"Okay, let's go," Zoe whispered. They hurried along the wall to the front door. But when Logan pushed down on the handle, the door didn't budge.

"No way," Blue said. He tried the handle, too.

Zoe glanced anxiously at the back door, where the flashlight was now scanning the vending machine. "Break a window?" she suggested halfheartedly.

Logan thought he'd rather spend the night in the library than do that. He reached into his pocket. The keys from the children's room were still there; he'd forgotten to put them back.

"Try this," he said, handing them to Blue.

"Oh," Zoe said, sounding a little exasperated. "Of course you have keys to the library. You didn't think that was worth mentioning before?"

"I just found them, I promise," Logan said as the key clicked in the lock. Blue pushed open the door, and they ran out and down the front steps. Logan grabbed the keys from Blue and slipped them into the book drop box at the edge of the sidewalk.

Footsteps crunched on dry leaves around the corner of the library. Whoever it was must have heard the front door and was coming fast.

Someone was about to catch them with the griffin cub.

FIFTEEN

Logan, Zoe, and Blue took off down the street.

Zoe clutched the griffin cub to her chest. She didn't dare look back. She'd had almost this exact nightmare too many times before. Whenever she looked back, that was when they always got her—and all the Menagerie animals—and everything was ruined forever.

But this time it was real.

She threw herself on her bike, leaving her helmet hanging from the handlebars, and flew out of the alley, nearly knocking over Blue and Logan. Flurp wriggled in protest, but Zoe wasn't going to stop until she was safely home.

She took a back route, just in case the person chasing

them had a car, although she hadn't heard one. She zipped through a narrow alley and detoured through a playground and around the elementary school. Flurp's claws dug through her shirt in little stabs of pain, but Zoe just gritted her teeth and kept going.

Finally she was pedaling up the hill to her own house. Now she let herself look back. The tall orange lights lit an empty street behind her.

The trees along her driveway felt like warm arms welcoming her in. The garage door was open, and as she rolled her bike inside, Matthew stood up from one of the golf carts, wiping his hands on a rag.

"Hey," he said. "I am so telling that you're not wearing your helmet." He squinted more closely. "Yikes. You look terrible."

"Always the best way to say hi," Zoe said. She dropped her bike and loosened the sling so Flurp could poke her head out. "But look who we found in the library!"

"Awesome!" Matthew bounded over and helped disentangle Flurp. His strong hands ran gently over her fur and wings, and not for the first time, Zoe wondered how he had ever made a griffin angry enough to claw his arm up. Matthew was great with the animals, a born Tracker, and the scars he'd brought back from training camp this past summer made no sense.

"Great work," Matthew said, tousling Zoe's hair. "You'll

be running this place soon."

Zoe just barely managed not to shudder. She loved most of the animals, but she wasn't at all sure she wanted to be the next Kahn caretaker. If the Menagerie stressed her out this much *now*, how much worse would it be if she were in charge of everything? And if she did have to inherit it—if Ruby followed her dream of being an actress and Matthew became a Tracker—then she'd really never get to have a normal life, not for one minute.

It wasn't fair, being the youngest.

"She's hungry," Zoe pointed out as Flurp nipped at Matthew's zipper. "She hasn't eaten all day, so make sure she gets something."

"I'll go reunite her with her delighted parents," Matthew said. "Well, her delighted parent and her semicomatose parent anyway." He carried Flurp out the back door of the garage just as Logan and Blue came riding up the driveway on their bikes.

"Were you followed?" Zoe asked. She peered out at the dark road behind them, beyond the trees. No headlights; no dark figure that she could see. But uneasiness clung to her thoughts like cobwebs.

"Doubt it," Blue said. "We were fast." He held out his hand, and, looking surprised, Logan high-fived him.

"Let's get inside and close up," Zoe said, reaching for the garage door button.

Out on the road there was a muffled engine rumble-cough, and a pair of headlights came swinging around the corner into the driveway.

Logan looked like he was about to grab a weapon. Zoe took his elbow and pulled him to the side wall. "It's okay," she said. "That's our van."

The Kahns' battered gray-blue van rolled into the garage, and she hit the button to close up behind it. The sound of the door thunking into the concrete made her feel a lot better. Now at least there was something between her and all the people who might destroy the Menagerie.

Her mother turned off the engine, but the van kept shaking, and now they could hear the muffled squawking coming from inside.

Logan put his hands over his ears. "Oh, *man*, she is *mad*," he said. He lowered his hands again and looked at them ruefully. "Of course that wasn't going to work."

So there's one upside to not being able to hear the griffin cubs, Zoe thought, but it didn't cheer her up.

Her dad climbed out of the passenger side, smiling. "Got one!" he said.

"So did we," Zoe said. She loved the look on her dad's face—proud but not surprised, as if he'd had no doubt she would come back with a griffin cub. "Matthew took her inside. Wait—wasn't Matthew supposed to go to the bank with you?"

"We couldn't find him," her dad said. "And we were in kind of a hurry. It's the big one, by the way." He lifted the smallest dragon harness off the wall and began tightening the straps to make it as small as possible.

"Do we really have to harness her?" Zoe asked.

"AWK AWK AWKAWKAWKAWK!" bellowed the unseen griffin cub. From the banging inside, Zoe could tell she was crashing her cage into the sides of the van.

"I think that's a yes," said Blue.

"I don't understand," Zoe's mom said, hopping out on the other side of the van. "Why isn't she happy to be home? We're all so nice to her here." Mom's hair was a mess, and there was a rip in her flowing daisy-patterned shirt, as if she'd tried to hug the cub and it had strongly objected.

"Well, escaping was her idea," Logan said in a strained voice. He had his hands to his head like he was trying to hold his skull together. "She's hollering 'MY TREASURE! MY BEAUTIFUL TREASURE!' over and over again. Plus some creative things about what she's going to do when she—"

A sudden silence made him stop midsentence.

They all stared at the van.

"That's good, right?" Zoe's mom said hopefully. "That means she's calmed—"

Scrabble. Scritch scratch scrabble scrabble. The sound of claws on metal . . . on the sides of the van itself. Which meant the griffin was not inside the cage anymore.

Scratch scratch scratch scratch SCRAAAATCH.

"Uh-oh," said Zoe's dad.

The black griffin cub exploded out of the van with such force that one of the back doors fell off, crashing loudly to the floor. She was the largest of the cubs, already the size of a small pony. In the confined garage, it was like a rocket set loose in a Looney Tunes cartoon, zooming wildly around the room.

Zoe threw herself to the floor, covering her head. Her parents and Blue did the same thing as the griffin shot from wall to wall with shrieks of anger. She slammed into the hooks of dragon harnesses and frantically clawed them all to the ground. One of her wings whacked into Logan and knocked him over as well. With another leap she landed on the tool cabinet, sending drawers of nuts and bolts and screws clattering into sharp metal puddles.

"AWK AWK AWKAWKAWK!" she roared, bounding onto the top of the van. She landed with a thud and a screech of claws on metal. Her wings brushed the ceiling, nearly blotting out the light from the single bulb.

Zoe was sure the griffin didn't mean to hurt any of them, but in her rage and in such a small space, she easily might by accident. They needed Matthew and his calming hands. Or a tranq gun . . . She raised her head a little to look at the gun chest on the far side of the room. Maybe if she could get to it. . . .

She began a slow army crawl, wriggling along the wall.

"AWKAWKAWKOOOOOAR!" the griffin cub howled. Zoe froze and glanced up. Glittering black eyes were fixed on her. The griffin spread her wings and hooked her claws over the edge of the van, ready to pounce.

"Clink!" yelled Logan. "Stop!"

SIXTEEN

The griffin swiveled her head around in surprise and stared at Logan.

"Clink," he said again. "That's your name, right?"

Lucky guess? the griffin wondered.

"No, I can hear you," Logan said, climbing to his feet. "Loud and clear." Clink's voice in his head vibrated like swords clashing.

Hear me? Clink flapped her wings. **Then GIVE ME! WANT! Treasure! Treasure! TREASURE!** She opened her beak and hissed at the Kahns. Her claws flexed menacingly, and they looked a lot more like full-grown lion paws than either Squorp's or Flurp's.

Logan did not want to see those claws sinking into Zoe's back or that beak stabbing at Blue's eyes. He could only think of one thing to do. "Here," he said, fighting past the lump rising in his throat. He reached into his pocket and pulled out his mom's bracelet. "I have some really important treasure for you to guard. Really, *really* important. You have to be very careful with it and . . . and make sure it never gets lost and . . ." He stopped, swallowing. Was he really giving Mom's bracelet away? To a bossy, aggressive four-month-old griffin cub?

Clink ducked her head to peer at the bracelet. The gold chain glinted in the light, and the twelve charms spun and winked. The one that looked like a bird with big eyes was staring at Logan accusingly. *Your mom gave this to you when she traveled. She told you to take care of it for her while she was gone. What if she comes looking for it?*

She won't. She's not coming back, Logan thought, remembering the postcard.

The griffin cub jumped down to the floor, landing on quiet cat feet. She sat on her haunches and neatly lifted the bracelet out of Logan's hand with one claw. The elephant charm glowed against her dark fur as she turned the bracelet cautiously from side to side.

Beautiful treasure, Clink breathed softly in Logan's mind. **So delicate. Very important to someone. Full of meaning.** Her black eyes were fierce and warm at the same time as she looked into Logan's face. *I will guard it with all the courage of my ancestors.*

Suddenly Logan didn't feel guilty anymore. He knew she meant it. She would be gentle and careful with it. Mom's bracelet would be safer with Clink than anywhere in the world.

"May I see that?" Mr. Kahn asked Clink. She snapped her beak and glared at him, covering the bracelet between her front paws.

"It's okay," Logan told her. "He's allowed."

May look but may not touch, insisted the griffin.

"She says you can look, but don't touch it," Logan explained. Mr. Kahn nodded, and the griffin proudly displayed the gold charm bracelet.

"Where did you get this?" Mr. Kahn asked Logan. From most adults the question would have sounded accusing, but he only seemed curious.

Logan wanted the Kahns to know it was okay for Clink to have it, but without making Clink think the bracelet wasn't important or worth guarding. "It was my mom's. She's not around anymore, so I need someone brave to guard it for me. Someone who knows it's special."

I do! Clink insisted, drawing herself up like a Greek statue. Her chest feathers ruffled proudly.

Mr. Kahn gave Clink a small, respectful bow. "We know you will take good care of it until Logan's mother returns, Clink."

Logan looked down at his sneakers, avoiding everyone's gaze. *Like that's ever going to happen.*

"Will you stay for dinner, Logan?" Mr. Kahn asked, resting one hand on Logan's shoulder. "It's just spaghetti, but I think you've more than earned it."

"*Just* spaghetti!" Mrs. Kahn protested. "I'll have you know I also defrosted turkey meatballs for you ungrateful lot."

Clink perked up, swiveling her head toward Zoe's mom.

"Yes, you can have a meatball," Mrs. Kahn said, smiling, "as long as you go back to your den without any more fussing."

No more fussing, Clink crooned. **Clink is a treasure guardian now.** She delicately draped the bracelet over a couple of large wing feathers and paced out of the garage, keeping one eye on the bracelet at all times.

"I'll go make sure that happens," Mrs. Kahn said. "Oh, and I'll let the dragons know they can add Logan to the welcome list so we won't get any intruder alarms during dinner." She hurried off.

"I just need to call my dad, but it should be fine," Logan said to Mr. Kahn. He felt lucky they weren't kicking him out yet. Even with the scary person at the library and losing his mom's bracelet, this was still the best day he'd had in Xanadu. The best day he'd had since Mom left, actually.

A side door in the garage led right into Zoe's kitchen.

It was huge and warm, with copper pots hanging from the ceiling, a mountain of mysterious gadgets piled on the drying rack by the sink, and two stoves crowded with covered saucepans. An herb garden was rioting in the bay window, effectively blocking the view of the driveway with winding green leaves and tiny red tomatoes. The room smelled like garlic bread and spaghetti sauce.

Logan nearly tripped over one of the hellhounds, who was lying sprawled across the heated, silvery gray stone floor. The large dog thumped his tail once and didn't even look up. Zoe frowned at him.

"Sheldon," she said, "can't you even *pretend* to be a scary guard dog?"

Sheldon panted cheerfully at her.

"You can call your dad in there," Blue said to Logan, pointing to an archway to the left. Beside it was a pass-through window to the next room, where Blue began stacking plates and mismatched silverware as Zoe handed them to him.

Logan went through the archway and found himself in a wide, open room. The quarter of it closest to the kitchen was a dining area filled with an enormous wooden table that looked like it had been a tree for a very long time. The surface was hacked and pitted like real wood, not smoothed over like most tables.

The rest of the space was a living room two steps down

from the dining room. It stretched all the way to the far wall of the house, taking up most of the ground floor. It was covered in thick carpets, woven wall hangings of mythical creatures, comfortable-looking couches, enormous, floppy floor pillows, and what appeared to be hundreds of books— shoved into bookcases or sprawled across low tables or tucked into the corners of overstuffed armchairs.

There was no TV, but there were two things against the tall, sliding glass doors that reminded Logan of the mounted binoculars on the Skydeck at the top of the Sears Tower. The windows all looked out on the dark Menagerie, down the rolling grass hills to the lake glittering in the moonlight.

Logan sat in one of the large wooden chairs around the table, suddenly feeling exhausted. He pulled out his phone and dialed his dad's cell.

As always when Logan called, Dad answered on the first ring.

"Hey, Logan," he said. "Sorry I'm not home yet."

"That's okay," Logan said. "Neither am I. One of my—" He stopped. It felt weird to say "friends." Blue and Zoe weren't exactly his friends yet, were they? He wondered what they would say about that. "This guy at school invited me for dinner," he said instead. "Is that okay?"

"Of course," said his dad, sounding relieved. "That's great, Logan. No problem at all. What's his name?"

"Blue," Logan answered. That seemed easier than trying to explain Zoe and her family. Besides, if his dad thought he was hanging out with a girl, he'd never hear the end of it.

His dad chuckled a little. "I've never met someone named Blue," he said. "Is he cool?"

"Yeah, obviously," Logan said, glancing at the pass-through with a grin. "Only the coolest people want to hang out with me." Blue slid a pitcher of iced tea onto the bar and grinned back at Logan.

"All right, have fun," said his dad. "I'll be home late, and out early tomorrow. But Sunday night, right? You, me, and the Bears?"

"You bet," Logan said. "I'll probably be out a lot tomorrow, too."

"With Blue?"

"Yeah, probably." He hoped he'd be out looking for griffins, anyhow. Actually, even if he wasn't invited, he wouldn't let that stop him. He could look for griffin cubs on his own if he had to.

"All right, stay safe and have fun. I'll check on you when I get home tonight."

"Don't work too hard," said Logan. It was what he always said, but it had felt different to say it after Mom left. Like he kind of meant it more than he did before.

He hung up and glanced out at the Menagerie. One of the unicorns trotted out of the stable and stopped by the side of the lake, tossing its head so its silver mane rippled. Logan got up and walked around the table toward the window, then stopped short with a gasp.

He'd noticed the pile of brown fur when he came in, but he'd thought it was some kind of shaggy rug. Now he could see that it wasn't.

In the middle of the floor, sleeping on one of the enormous, pumpkin-colored pillows, was a woolly mammoth.

SEVENTEEN

Zoe leaned against the kitchen counter and closed her eyes for a moment. Half the griffin cubs were back, but she certainly didn't feel half as stressed. *Either I left the gate unlocked by accident or someone snuck over to the enclosure later and unlocked it on purpose.*

She wasn't even sure which one she wanted to be true.

"ZOE!" Keiko called from upstairs. "I know you're down there! Your stupid Skype is like FREAKING OUT! Get up here and turn it off!"

"It must be Ruby," Dad said, looking up from the grapes he was chopping for the salad. "Tell her we said hi, and no, it's totally fine that she never Skypes or emails *us*, and we look forward to her next call when she runs out of money for all those textbooks she'll never read."

"Do I have to talk to her?" Zoe sighed. "Last time she spent the whole call explaining why even a senile basilisk would appreciate it if I wore heels now and then."

"I'll finish setting the table," Blue said with his lucky-to-be-an-only-child grin.

Zoe hurried up the stairs. She could hear Skype pinging and blooping away on her laptop. In their room, Keiko was sprawled across her own bed, glaring at her math homework. Her long braids were clipped up so they looked like two extra ears on top of her head.

"Shut that thing up," Keiko snapped.

"My day was great, thanks," Zoe said. "And yours?"

"Oh, witty," Keiko said. "And original. Like your fashion sense." She closed her math book and pointedly stalked out of the room.

Thank you SO much, universe, for giving me TWO impossible sisters. Zoe sat down at her desk and clicked on the ANSWER WITH VIDEO button. Immediately Ruby's face popped onto the screen, leaning in toward the camera. Ruby's eyes were fixed on the lower corner of her screen, where she could see herself on video, and she kept adjusting her head tilt to look as cute as possible.

"Hi, Ruby," Zoe said, trying to sound upbeat. "Hey, your hair is blond again." Ruby's asymmetrical pixie cut peaked on one side of her head. Heart-shaped rubies dangled from her ears, and a tiny ruby glittered in her nose. Zoe knew the earrings had been a present from Jonathan on Ruby's seventeenth birthday, but the epic tragedy of their relationship apparently hadn't stopped Ruby from wearing them.

"Zoe, what did you DO?" Ruby demanded. She squinted at the video screen. "And are you wearing flannel again? Didn't we talk about this?"

"We're about to have dinner, Ruby, so—"

"Stop right there," Ruby said. "Dinner? How can you even think about having dinner when those griffin cubs are out there?"

Zoe took a deep, calming breath that didn't calm her down at all. There was only one person who would have told Ruby about the missing griffins. *Matthew, why would you do this to me?* "It's okay," she said. "We've got three of them back already."

"Yeah?" Ruby checked her teeth and rubbed a bit of lipstick off one of them. "Where were they?"

"The library, the bank, and—" Zoe couldn't think of a lie fast enough. "And this guy Logan's house."

"Who's that?" Ruby asked. "Logan? He didn't see anything, did he?"

"He's just a guy in my class," Zoe said. "Um. He's . . . kind of helping us. He can hear the griffin cubs, Ruby. It's pretty amazing."

"Oh, no," Ruby said, jabbing her finger at the screen. "No, sir. You know the rules, Zoe! I don't care how cute he is. You don't want to get your heart broken like mine, do you?"

Zoe was really, tremendously over hearing about Ruby's heartbreak. "I never said he was cute!" she protested. "It's not like that. I barely know him. He's been useful, that's all."

"But you're not going to let him leave knowing about the Menagerie, are you?"

That's ironic. Ironic and unfair, Zoe thought bitterly.

"Ruby, I have to go to dinner." She reached for the mouse.

"ZOE!" Ruby yelled. "Do you have any idea what's at stake here? Do you know what'll happen if SNAPA finds out those cubs got loose?"

"Of course I do," Zoe said. "They'll shut down the Menagerie. I don't want that, either, Ruby." It was true—as much as she sometimes wished for a normal life, she would never risk the Menagerie for anything.

"It's not just that," Ruby said, a little triumphantly. "Mom and Dad don't want you to know, but I think you should. Ever since that whole thing in the Amazon last year, SNAPA policy is to terminate any escaped creatures on sight."

Zoe froze with one hand on the mouse. She felt like all the air had been sucked out of her.

"Exterminators?" she said. "You mean they're real?"

"All I know is the new policy," Ruby said. "If they find any griffin cubs outside the walls, they'll kill them. They might even kill the ones you already brought back, to make sure they don't cause trouble again."

"That doesn't make sense," Zoe cried. "They're a *protection* agency! It's right there in the name."

"Protecting the secret of all the animals is more important than keeping one or two alive," Ruby said, shaking her head so the earrings flashed. "And if they find out about your boyfriend, it'll be much worse. Who knows what they might do to him? I totally understand your feelings, Zoe, but you have to be strong, like I was."

"It's nothing like Jonathan," Zoe said, irritated. "Logan is just a friend." *And he's not an enormous thieving jerk, either.*

"You can talk to me, Zoe," Ruby said. She tilted her head and put on her concerned older-sister expression. "Obviously I understand what you're going through better than anyone."

"You really, really do not," Zoe said.

"Well, okay," Ruby said. "I mean, *I* never lost any of the Menagerie animals, so *that* part I can't relate to, but I do know what it's like to give up something you love." She sighed dramatically.

"GOOD-BYE, RUBY." Zoe clicked off before Ruby could make her feel worse, and then closed her laptop so Ruby couldn't call back.

Was it true? Would SNAPA kill the griffin cubs if the agents found out they'd escaped? Zoe rubbed at her temples, trying to erase her headache. And what would they do if they found out about Logan? Or what if Logan went home tonight and told someone about the griffins, even after promising he wouldn't? How much did she really know about this guy anyway? Could they trust him with something so important?

She went slowly back down the stairs, studying her dad from above. He'd been acting surprisingly calm about the griffin escape—he and Mom had been so busy with all the other SNAPA fixes they had to get done—but now that she looked, she could see that his hair had gotten crazier as the day went on, which was always a bad sign. It poked up in wild tufts all over his head, and he wasn't whistling over the salad like he normally would be.

She glanced at the bread box, and then out at Logan, who was talking to Blue in the living room.

I like him, but he's a liability, she thought. *Like Jonathan. As long as he knows about the Menagerie, everything here is in danger.*

Maybe I can't get the griffin cubs back right now . . . but at least there's one thing I can do to protect us all.

EIGHTEEN

"I know what you're thinking," Blue said, appearing at Logan's elbow. "You're thinking, 'Wait, a mammoth's not a mythical creature.'"

"Way too advanced," Logan said. "My brain's stuck back at 'Hey, there's a mammoth on the floor.'" His skin prickled with excitement. "I should ask you guys for a list so I won't keep being surprised by everything." Blue laughed.

The mammoth snorted and rolled sideways so its trunk flopped over the edge of the pillow. A small, honey-colored tusk poked out on either side of its trunk, and a furry tuft of brown hair hung over its eyes.

"All right, wait," said Logan. "A mammoth's not a mythical

creature. They really existed, like, forever ago. Didn't they?"

"Yup," Blue said. "One of our best Trackers rescued him from some kind of cloning lab when he was only a month or two old. I mean, where else are you going to put a mammoth, right? I guess the Tracker thought the lab wasn't safe for him."

"That's not a full-grown mammoth, is it?" Logan asked. From what he could tell, the animal on the floor was bigger than a horse, but not as big as he'd imagined a mammoth would be.

"Nah, the Captain's only two years old," Blue answered. "He's not even elephant-sized yet. It is not going to be fun the day he crashes through the stairs and we have to explain why he can't come sleep in the house anymore."

Zoe came in with the glasses and began to set them around the table. "Zoe's his favorite," Blue added.

Zoe's tense expression relaxed, and she grinned at the sleeping pile of mammoth. "He's the best animal in the Menagerie," she said. She put the last glass in place, hopped down into the living room, and knelt beside the mammoth. He wriggled closer to her, half dozing as she rubbed his side vigorously. In seconds her jeans were covered in long, brown hairs.

"Oh, hey," Logan said. Now he recognized the smell in the room competing with the warm-food scents from the kitchen. "That's what your——" He stopped. Maybe it wasn't the best move to tell Zoe how weird her backpack smelled.

Zoe brushed at the fur on her hands with a rueful look. "I know; I'm always covered in this stuff although I roller my clothes like ten times a day." She shrugged and hugged the mammoth. "Captain Fuzzbutt is worth it, though."

Logan couldn't help but agree. He wouldn't care *what* he smelled like if he had something like this waiting for him at home.

Captain Fuzzbutt lifted his head and shook it like a dog, his ears flapping. He opened large brown eyes and raised his trunk to poke Zoe's face. The soft end felt around for a minute, then lifted up in the air and turned like a periscope, twitching as if it was sniffing. His head flopped back down, and he rolled his eyes toward the boys.

His gaze landed on Logan and stopped. Suddenly the mammoth bolted to his feet, knocking Zoe sideways. The Captain stared at Logan for another moment, and then, all at once, he charged.

"Fuzzbutt!" Zoe shouted. "Stop!"

Logan only had a moment to see the sharp tusks coming at him and wonder if he'd be the first person in ten thousand years to be killed by a woolly mammoth. A second later he felt the furry trunk circle his waist and lift him straight off the ground. The room revolved as the mammoth rolled him in, and Logan ended up eye to eye with Captain Fuzzbutt.

His fear melted away. The mammoth's expression was clearly delighted.

"Captain Fuzzbutt! Let him go before I demote you," Zoe commanded. "That's no way to treat a guest."

Logan was swept with a new wave of dizziness as the creature lowered him back to the floor. The mammoth's trunk patted Logan down, as though making sure he hadn't done any damage. It stopped at Logan's hand and poked his palm.

Logan laughed and held out his fist. The mammoth bumped it gently with the end of his trunk.

"Huh," Mr. Kahn said from the kitchen doorway. "I've only seen him do that once before."

Zoe kicked the carpet. "I've never seen him do that. Fuzzbutt is usually totally shy around strangers. I guess you have a special bond with mammoths, too, griffin whisperer."

"Cool," Logan said, reaching up to rub the Captain's forehead between his eyes. He estimated the mammoth was about six feet tall, the same height as both his mom and his dad. Fuzzbutt rumbled low in his throat and patted Logan's forehead with his trunk.

"Yeah," Zoe said. " 'Cool.' Now you just have to sweet-talk the kelpie. If *she* decides not to eat you, I'm seriously quitting this family and moving to New York."

"What's a kelpie?" Logan asked nervously.

"Don't ask," said Blue. "Better if you never meet her. She's nastier than the unicorns."

"And a smidge more murder-y," Zoe said, squeezing past

the mammoth to get back to the table. "But that's how kelpies are."

"Nonsense." Zoe's mom caught the tail end of the conversation as she came through the sliding door from the garden. "She just needs a little more positive-rewards-based training, that's all." The weird chirruping night noises of the Menagerie disappeared again as she thunked the door shut.

Zoe rolled her eyes at Logan. "You sit there," she said, pointing to the chair opposite hers. Logan obeyed, and the mammoth flopped down next to him with a thump that made the whole house shake.

Logan's glass of iced tea was already poured, but as he reached for it, Blue offered him the platter of garlic bread. Then there was salad and two giant bowls of pasta, one with meatballs and one without. He noticed that Zoe and her dad took the pasta without meatballs.

"Keiko!" Zoe's mom yelled in the general direction of the front hall. "Dinner!"

"I'm not hungry!" a voice shouted from upstairs. Logan remembered the bad-tempered sixth grader who had been with Zoe and Blue earlier that day.

"Keiko lives here, too?" he asked.

"We adopted her last year," Zoe said. "Yay."

"Zoe," her father said sternly.

"What?" she replied. "I said yay."

"There are turkey meatballs!" Mrs. Kahn called sweetly.

"I hate turkey meatballs!" Keiko shouted back.

Mrs. Kahn sighed. Blue hid a smile.

"She'll eat when she's hungry," said Zoe's dad calmly. "Unlike Melissa, who could probably starve to death over her calculator and not even notice." He unclipped a walkie-talkie from his belt and spoke into it. "Melissa, put down Form B7504 and get in here."

The walkie-talkie crackled, and a female voice said, "Form B7504? Who's been eaten by a grindylow, and why don't I know about this?"

"I was joking, Melissa," Zoe's father answered. "Dinner is ready."

"Well, that's hardly the same thing," Melissa's voice responded. "Please refrain from joking about forms in the future. Form B7504 is particularly complicated, with several subsections."

Blue and Zoe exchanged amused looks. Logan jumped as a door opened on the far side of the living room. The blond woman in the perfect suit and pearls came out, still looking as neatly put together as she had earlier that day. She clipped across the carpets in her heels, studying a piece of paper in her hand, and nearly bumped into Matthew as he came through the sliding doors.

"The unicorns are out for their moonlight gallop," Zoe's brother reported. "And Nero is fully reborn and back to flapping around complaining about his accommodations. He wanted you all to see his new finery, though, so I let him out for a minute." He pointed toward the window.

The phoenix came strutting past the glass, head held high, looking extremely pleased with himself.

Logan did a double take. The phoenix was wearing a miniature dark-blue hooded jacket that looked suspiciously familiar, apart from being bird sized.

Matthew and Blue hooted with laughter. "I had no idea that would happen," Matthew said, wiping his eyes. "But it's awesome. And he loves it, if that's any consolation," he added to Logan.

It sort of was, actually, Logan had to admit to himself. The phoenix swept off back to the Aviary, preening as he went.

Matthew sat down next to Zoe and helped himself to half the meatballs. "Also, Scratch ate hardly any of his dinner again, but he says he's feeling fine."

Zoe pulled out a small notebook and wrote something Logan couldn't decipher; it looked like a string of triangles and squiggles, on a long list of other triangles and squiggles.

"Hi, Mom," Blue said, pulling out the chair beside him. Melissa finally looked up from her paper and leaned in to kiss the top of his head. She froze, staring at Logan.

"Dear God," she said. "That's not Keiko."

"It's not?" Blue said, pretending to sound shocked. "It looks just like her! Hey, you, how did you get in here?"

"This isn't funny, Blue," Melissa said as Logan quickly swallowed his laugh. "You know the rules about inviting friends home." Her gaze drifted down to the mammoth sprawled across the floor, and her eyes widened. She made a face at the Kahns, like *The mammoth is right there! He's going to notice it any second!*

"It's okay, Mom," Blue said, tugging her into her seat. "This is Logan. Logan, this is my mom. He knows about the Menagerie. He's helping us find the griffins."

"What?" Melissa popped right back up again. "But the forms! The confidentiality agreement! The outsider-inclusion-and-intruder-override application! The background check!" She pressed her hands to her perfectly smooth hair. "We're in enough trouble with SNAPA. If they find *him* here on Sunday . . ."

"Relax, Mom. He's helped us get three of the cubs back already," Blue said.

"Well, I hardly—" Logan started, and Zoe kicked him under the table.

Melissa sat down, looking a little less panic-stricken. "Really? Three already. That's promising." She served herself a bowl of salad and then picked out all the cucumbers with her fork, carefully putting them in a separate bowl. Blue had done the same thing, Logan noticed.

"Sorry about this, Logan," said Mrs. Kahn, "but we have to go over our SNAPA list during dinner." Logan realized everyone had a notebook next to his or her plate except for him and Blue.

"There's a lot to get done before Sunday," Mr. Kahn said, rubbing his forehead exactly the way Zoe always did. "Somebody please tell me you fixed the security camera over the roc's nest today."

He sighed into the silence and made a note. "I'll do it after dinner."

Logan reached for his iced tea. A bowl of shredded cheese intercepted his hand halfway.

"The sauce is even better with cheese," Blue insisted. "Seriously, try it."

"Okay," Logan said. He looked across the table as he sprinkled the cheese and noticed Zoe staring at him and Blue oddly. "SNAPA seems kind of scary," he offered.

"Oh, yeah," Blue said. "Lots of rules, especially for merpeople."

"Rules are there for the protection of the animals *and* humanity," said Melissa.

"But even you have to admit not all of this seems necessary," said Zoe's mom, waving her notebook. "They're being unreasonably hard on us, considering the jackalope is perfectly safe and sound."

"Like the den for the Chinese dragon we never got," Matthew said through a mouthful of spaghetti. "It's only been a few months since we were expecting it, after all. I don't understand why we have to convert that space into something else already."

"SNAPA doesn't like us much," Zoe said glumly.

Melissa shook her head. "And if they find out about the griffin escape, they will shut us down with no hesitation." She took one meatball and started slicing it into small pieces in her salad.

Shut down the Menagerie? Logan's heart sank. But he'd just found them. He couldn't imagine going back to normal life now that he knew griffins and unicorns and dragons were out there somewhere.

"Didn't something like that happen in the Amazon?" Zoe asked Melissa. Her dad gave Zoe a sharp look.

"Oh, yes." Melissa took a tiny bite of tomato. "It was terrible. One of the dragons went mad and killed a couple of people. It only takes one bad creature to ruin everything. The whole place had to be closed. You can't *imagine* the paperwork that must have been involved."

"What happened to the rest of the animals?" Zoe pressed.

"Who's ready for dessert?" Zoe's dad stood up in a hurry. "Pear cobbler, anyone?"

"Well, of course they terminated half of them," Melissa said, focused on her salad. "If they were too big to move or too much trouble. Only the most endangered ones can be saved after something like that. Here, for instance, the phoenix and the goose and the kraken would be worth saving, but probably not the griffins or the dragons."

Logan stared at her. She didn't really mean *terminate*, did she?

Melissa looked up at the silence with a surprised expression.

"So it is true! Dad!" Zoe dropped her knife and fork on the plate with a clatter. "How could you not tell me?"

"We thought you were worried enough," her mom said, giving Melissa a withering look.

"Well, you should be *more* worried!" Zoe said. "I didn't know any of the animals might *die*! We should be out looking for them right now!" She sounded like she was about to cry.

Logan's throat felt like it was closing up. The griffin cubs—Squorp and Flurp and Clink—how could anyone do anything to harm them? He grabbed his iced tea and lifted it to his mouth.

Suddenly the glass was knocked out of his hand. Purplish-brown tea spilled across his pants and splashed on the mammoth below him. Fuzzbutt looked up, startled, as Logan leaped to his feet with a yell.

"Blue, what on earth was that?" Melissa said, shocked.

Logan blinked down at the blond boy who was pointing at Zoe accusingly.

"I know what you were about to do," Blue said. "And it's not okay with me." He met Logan's eyes. "Sorry, Logan. Zoe was just about to wipe your memory."

NINETEEN

"Zoe!" her mom gasped.

"Blue!" Melissa set down her fork and frowned at him. "We never, *never* talk about that in front of outsiders."

Logan's head was spinning. He felt confused and betrayed and also very wet. "You're not serious," he said to Blue. "You can't really do that, can you? Wipe my memory—like in *Men in Black*?"

"A lot like that," Blue said. "But with kraken ink instead of alien technology."

"Blue!" Melissa stood up. "That is enough! Go to your room *right now*."

"I will, but I'm taking Logan with me," Blue said. "Come

on, I'll lend you some dry pants." He stood up, giving Zoe a challenging look. She buried her face in her hands.

"It's all right, Melissa," Mr. Kahn said. "Zoe. This is serious."

Logan didn't know what to say as he followed Blue through the kitchen to the wide staircase in the front hall. His sneakers squished and his pants stuck to his legs. "This place seems determined to ruin my clothes," he tried to joke.

"My advice," Blue said, "is, don't drink anything but water while you're here. If someone puts kraken ink in it, it'll turn purple." He paused thoughtfully, then added, "So, you know, don't drink any purple water." He was carrying the bowl of cucumbers he and Melissa had picked out of their salads.

"Why would Zoe do that to me?" Logan said. He stopped at the top of the stairs, clenching and unclenching his fists. Anger was starting to build in his chest. He hadn't done anything to betray their trust. He'd helped as much as he possibly could. He'd brought Squorp back instead of keeping him. He'd given Clink his mother's bracelet, for crying out loud.

"It's what we always do," Blue said. "It's Menagerie policy. But you're different, I think." He shook his hair out of his eyes and checked one of the small video screens that hung at eye level all the way along the hall, where family photos might be in any other house. The only thing Logan could see on the screen was a large, dark blob with small bubbles blipping out of it; underneath the screen was a printed label that said KRAKEN MONITORING SYSTEM. Blue nodded in satis-faction, opened the door next to the screen, and beckoned Logan after him.

Blue's room was both totally normal and weirdly Blue at the same time. The walls were painted a muted aqua color, and the carpet was shaggy and dark green like seaweed. Brightly colored glass fish hung from the ceiling like model airplanes. On the wall above the bed was a poster of Michael Phelps swimming, with water flying out around him. The opposite wall held a bulletin board crammed with deep-sea photographs of underwater life, which Logan realized Blue had probably taken himself. A few more photos were hung around the walls in plain black frames with labels on them such as MADAGASCAR and GREAT BARRIER REEF.

Bubbles and small white sea horses drifted across the computer monitor on the desk. *The Crucible* was stacked on top of a couple of books about Thomas Jefferson. Next to the computer was a framed photograph of Melissa with a tall, green-haired, bearded man on a beach somewhere. It took Logan a moment to recognize her, because Melissa's hair was down and she was laughing. The green-haired man was helping a blond toddler walk with his feet in the sand.

Blue set down the cucumbers next to a giant fish tank on a low bookshelf in the corner. The tank was half as tall as Logan and dark inside. Blue reached for a light switch hooked up to it, but before he could turn it on, Logan saw a small green hand with webbed fingers press up against the glass. It scrabbled at the side nearest the cucumbers.

"Oh," Blue said, pausing to look at Logan. "Uh, don't be freaked out. It's just a kappa. Okay?"

"A what?"

The light flicked on, illuminating the water in the tank and the tall, waving seaweed plants inside. Peering out through the dark fronds was a face. Logan jumped back in surprise, and the face grinned wolfishly.

The creature in the tank was the size of a skinny one-year-old and covered in green scales. Its body was blobby, like a frog's, but with a turtle shell on its back, and its monkey face had a beak—a beak with sharp little teeth. There was a tiny crater on the top of its skull. It poked at the glass again, ogling the cucumbers.

"Don't get too close," Blue said. "Kappas eat kids, but they prefer cucumbers if they can get them."

"That—that would *eat* me?" Logan said, fascinated. "But it's so small."

"Yeah, it's stronger than it looks," Blue said. "If it ever asks you to wrestle, seriously, just say no." He slipped two slices of cucumber through a slot at the top of the tank. The kappa reached its webbed fingers up and snatched a cucumber out of the water, making it disappear in two bites.

"Of course," Blue went on, "you won't understand it if it

does talk to you. It only speaks Japanese. Sometimes Keiko talks to it, but I'm pretty sure she's just riling it up." He dropped a few more cucumber slices in and crossed over to his closet. The kappa stared at Logan with mischievous dark eyes.

"You said it's Menagerie policy to wipe people's memories," Logan said. "You mean everyone? You do this all the time?"

"Well, we don't get strangers in here very much," Blue said. "So not *all* the time, but whenever it happens, yeah." He pulled a pair of jeans off a shelf in the closet and threw them at Logan. "Try those."

"And you don't warn them?" Logan asked, kicking off his shoes. "You just take their memories, like that?" It gave him the creeps to think of anyone messing with his head. Would he still have remembered his dad—or anything about his mom?

Blue went back to throwing cucumbers into the kappa's tank. "It's not like we give them total amnesia," he said. "The kraken ink targets supernatural encounters. The more you've had, the more you need. You've only been around a day, so a couple of drops would have you waking up tomorrow with this fuzzy feeling, like you'd slept through a whole afternoon. You might remember going to the library, but not why, and definitely not the griffin cubs or the Menagerie."

"What about my mom's bracelet?" Logan burst out. "Would Zoe have given it back? Or would she have left me thinking I lost it somewhere?"

Blue shoved his blond hair off his forehead and gave Logan a rueful look. "I don't know. Listen, we don't like the policy. But it's to keep the Menagerie safe."

"You don't have to keep it safe from *me*," Logan protested. "I want to help. I would never tell anyone."

"I believe you." Both boys jumped, and Logan spun around to find Zoe standing in the doorway, holding her elbows and looking downcast. He was glad he'd gotten the jeans on before she appeared. Assuming she hadn't been standing there for a while. He frowned at her.

"I mean, I *want* to believe you," Zoe said. "But the Menagerie is in so much trouble right now. I just . . . Don't you get it?"

"Not cool," Logan said, pointing at her. He sat down on Blue's bed.

But the problem was, he *did* understand. He already felt like he'd do almost anything to protect the griffins and this place. In his mind, though, that included Zoe and Blue. He'd thought they were starting to be a team. Or friends, or something.

But friends didn't wipe other friends' memories.

"I'm really sorry," Zoe said. She rubbed her forehead. "Dad is pretty angry. He says we need you. I know he's right, it's just—my sister got me all scared. The last time we let a stranger come in and out of the Menagerie . . . well, we thought we could trust him, too, and it turned out we really couldn't, and lots of things went wrong from there."

"How about this," Blue said. "What if Logan stays over tonight? Then he can help us hunt for griffins tomorrow, and we can all keep an eye on him to make sure he doesn't go home and sell our story to the dragon-conspiracy blogs." He tossed a cucumber slice at Logan. "You up for that? Saturday is Zoe's day to make breakfast."

Logan caught the cucumber and lobbed it at Zoe. She ducked, and it hit the hallway wall with a splat. "How do I know you won't wipe my brain while I'm sleeping?" Logan asked.

"Because that's impossible," Zoe said huffily.

"Hmm," Logan said. "Not a reassuring answer."

"And you've got my word," Blue said. He crossed the room and held out his hand to Logan. "Merman's honor. I won't let anyone wipe your memory unless you become a true danger to this place."

Logan looked over at Zoe. She nodded, kicking the carpet with her sneakers.

"All right," Logan said, shaking Blue's hand. He knew his dad would let him stay over. And despite the wrenched, horrible feeling in his stomach about what Zoe had tried to do to him, he still wanted to be here. He wanted to meet dragons. He wanted to hang out with Blue.

But more important than anything else, he had to help save Squorp and the other griffins.

TWENTY

"EWW!" A shriek woke Logan early the next morning. He squinted at the shades on Blue's window. It was still dark outside.

"Who left a CUCUMBER in the hallway?" Keiko's voice roared. "Where anyone could STEP ON IT. GROOOOOOSS!"

"Uh-oh," Blue whispered over the side of the bed. "Pretend you're still asleep."

Logan pulled the sleeping bag over his head as Blue's bedroom door slammed open.

"I know this is yours, fish boy," Keiko snapped, flinging the cucumber slice at Blue's head. Logan hadn't actually seen her the night before, but he knew she knew he was here. She didn't seem remotely interested in his existence.

"Sorry," Blue mumbled sleepily.

Keiko growled and slammed the door behind her.

"Maybe we should get up anyway," Logan suggested. "We could do something else on the SNAPA list, or start looking for griffins." Blue's alarm clock said 6:42 a.m., which was a horrible hour to be awake. But Logan hadn't slept well, and he felt restless.

"Mmmmph," Blue answered, burying his head under the pillow.

Logan slid out of the sleeping bag, put on the jeans and sweatshirt he'd borrowed from Blue, and crept into the hallway. Keiko had vanished, but the sound of the shower running came from under the bathroom door. No one else was around. All the other rooms were dark.

They'd all been up late working on SNAPA's list. Logan hadn't even seen Matthew or Mrs. Kahn come back before he and Blue went to sleep. Zoe had been sent off to bathe, brush, and feed something called a mapinguari, which she seemed to think she deserved. Logan had spent the evening helping Blue hammer a new roof on the Doghouse, where the hellhounds slept, next to the main house. All four hellhounds sat panting and staring at them with bright red eyes the whole time they were working.

He walked toward the stairs, peering at the video screens

as he went. One of them showed the griffin enclosure, where Squorp and Flurp were sleeping flopped over their mother's back. Nira kept shifting uncomfortably, but they only burrowed in more deeply. Riff was sprawled in front of the gate as if to block anyone from coming in or out.

Clink sat in the cave entrance, looking fierce and snapping at any leaves that dared to fall near her. Logan smiled. He wondered if she'd been awake all night guarding the bracelet, and whether she ever intended to sleep again.

He found his shoes and socks in the dryer in the kitchen closet and pulled them on. Captain Fuzzbutt wasn't in the living room—Logan had heard some gargantuan snores coming from Zoe's room, so he was pretty sure that's where the mammoth was. He stepped over the pillows and rugs and slid open one of the glass doors to the Menagerie.

Outside, the air felt chilly and gray and blurry in that before-sunrise kind of way. Logan rubbed his eyes and walked down toward the lake. Cleopatra and Charlemagne were standing at the edge of the water, drinking. They lifted their heads to stare at him, their horns glowing silvery pale in the dawn light.

Logan remembered what they'd said yesterday and bowed deeply. The unicorns glanced at each other with arch, pleased expressions, then both gave him a regal nod in return.

He followed the path around to the griffin enclosure

and stood looking at the bolts on the gate for a moment. It wouldn't be hard to unlock them from the outside—anyone could do it. But who would have?

He wanted to go inside, but he didn't want to cause any trouble that might get his memory wiped. So he circled the enclosure until he found a boulder close enough to it that he could climb up and rest his elbows on the top of the fence.

Clink's head instantly swiveled toward him with a beady-eyed glare. When she saw who it was, she relaxed and waved her tail.

Treasure is safe, small human, she said. **Not to worry.**

"I know," Logan said, giving her a thumbs-up. Small human! He wasn't short at all compared to most guys his age, although it was kind of embarrassing that he had to roll up the bottoms of Blue's jeans. But anyone would be short next to Blue.

"*Pssst*," Logan called softly, trying not to wake Nira or Riff. "Squorp!"

The tawny griffin cub stretched sleepily and dug his claws into his mother's fur. She wriggled and spread her wings, knocking him to the ground. Squorp rolled over and sat up with a startled expression. His feathers stuck out all around his face, and his fur was rumpled. Logan waved.

Logan! Squorp shook himself like a puppy and bounded over to the fence. **Missed you!** He jumped up and down, flapping his wings so Logan could reach the top of his head to scratch it. **Did you bring cow?**

"Sorry, buddy, no cow," Logan said. "I missed you, too, though."

Oh WAIT! Squorp cried. He stopped jumping and sat down to give Logan a stern look. **Squorp mad at you.**

"Mad at me?" Logan said. "Why? I'm sorry I didn't bring cow. I'll try to next time."

Not about cow! Squorp lashed his tail. He tilted his sharp beak toward Clink. **FIRST you bring back Bossy Bossy. What? Not sensible. Much more fun without her here! And THEN . . .** He paused dramatically, his chest swelling with outrage. **THEN Logan give CLINK treasure INSTEAD OF SQUORP.** The griffin clacked his beak furiously. **Very treasure Squorp found! Where SQUORP treasure, Logan? WHERE SQUORP TREASURE?**

"I'm sorry, Squorp," Logan said. He leaned over the fence, but Squorp took a step back, lifting his chin indignantly. "I'll find you some treasure, okay? Some really great treasure. I promise."

Hrrrrrrmph, said Squorp.

"Especially if you help me find the other cubs," Logan said. "What can you tell me about the griffins who are still missing?"

Squorp hesitated, as if he wanted to stay mad but couldn't

resist talking about his brothers and sisters.

"You could be the hero, Squorp," Logan said. He remembered the feathers on the post office steps the day before. "One of them is dark brown, right?"

Squorp snorted violently, his feathers flapping up and down. **That Clonk! Pfft. Clonk want so badly to be Clink. Super major big copycat.** He rolled his eyes.

"Do you know where Clonk went when you split up?" Logan asked.

Squorp shook his head. **Tried to follow Clink, but she bit him. Poor Clonk. Not very cool. Not like Squorp.**

"You are pretty cool," Logan agreed. "What about the other two? What do they look like? Have they picked their names yet?"

No, still deciding. Little gray sister, very clever. Too clever. Always thinking instead of eating or playing. Not natural.

"What kind of treasure would she like?" Logan asked.

Anything secret, Squorp said. **Most secret best treasure in town, probably.**

Logan rubbed his head, thinking. Where would there be secret treasure in a town like Xanadu?

"And the last griffin?" he asked.

Red brother, Squorp said. **Lots of fun, except at food time.** He spread his wings as wide as they would go. **Always hungry! Takes all the food! No good at sharing! Likes cow EVEN MORE than Squorp.** He eyed Logan beadily. **Logan better not give him SQUORP'S cow.**

"Don't worry," Logan said with a grin. "I will bring you masses of hamburger for this. Totally helpful, Squorp."

Squorp preened, smoothing his head feathers with one claw. **Squorp very helpful.**

"Yes, you are," Logan said. "You're magnificent."

Squorp MAGNIFICENT.

"If you think of anything else that might help, let me know, okay?" Logan said. "I'll come back later today if I can. But I'd better get back to the house before anyone finds me missing."

Bye, Logan! Come back soon! With treasure and cow! Squorp flapped his wings and bounced over to his mother, looking hungry.

Oops, Logan thought. *Poor Nira.* He got down from the boulder in a hurry so he wouldn't be the first thing the grumpy white griffin saw when she woke up. He was pretty sure she wouldn't be pleased that he'd woken Squorp so early.

As he walked back to the lake, something odd happened. It was hard for Logan to describe—it felt like a large shadow passing overhead, along with a gust of hot wind. But when he looked up, there was nothing in the gray sky above him.

"Huh," he said to himself. He could hear Pelly honking inside the Aviary and low rumbles coming from the mountain dens, which he assumed were the sounds of the three dragons waking up. Part of him was really tempted to go looking for them right now, before anyone could wipe his memory and he lost his chance forever. But he had a feeling that wandering into dragon dens uninvited was probably a bad idea.

He glanced up at the house and saw a light on in one of the upper windows. Somebody was up. Time to head back.

But when he glanced down again, he saw something standing on the shore of the lake—something he hadn't noticed before.

It looked like an ordinary horse. Its coat was grayish black, and water poured off its dripping black mane. It had enormous soft dark eyes, which were watching Logan in a way that seemed to say *I understand you. You're the friend I've been waiting for my whole life.*

"Wow," Logan said softly. It was like those eyes were calling to him. He approached cautiously, holding out one hand. The horse nickered, low and gentle.

Logan guessed this was like the normal birds in the Aviary—a regular horse to keep the unicorns company, or for the Kahns to ride around the Menagerie wherever the golf carts couldn't go.

The horse reached forward and nuzzled Logan's cupped

hand. Its nose was warm and velvety, even though it was wet.

"Have you been swimming?" Logan asked in a low voice. The horse's eyes met his, like it understood every word he said. He felt a small burst of happiness in his chest. He really was great with the Menagerie creatures—it was like he connected with them just as well as he did with his own pets. Surely Zoe wouldn't want to get rid of him once she realized he belonged here.

The horse sidled closer, as if it was offering its back to Logan. It turned its head to give him another meaningful look.

"Really?" Logan said. "You want me to ride you?"

The horse made a friendly whuffling sound and shook its mane at him.

Logan couldn't resist. Maybe it wanted to show him something important. And there was a rock right at Logan's feet, in the perfect spot for climbing up.

"Okay," Logan said. "Time for me to finally be a cowboy, right?"

He grasped the horse's mane and swung one leg over its back.

A roar of thunder boomed in Logan's ears as soon as he landed on the horse, as if he were in the middle of a storm cloud. The horse leaped forward into the lake in one mighty jump.

Logan yelled with alarm and then choked as the water closed over his head, pouring into his mouth. He let go of the horse's mane and tried to push away from it, to swim to the surface.

But he was *stuck to the horse's back.*

A magical force kept him pinned in place as the horse sank lower and lower—away from the air, away from the sky.

Logan was drowning.

TWENTY-ONE

Z oe hit the bedroom floor with a thump. A furry trunk jabbed her insistently in the face.

"Ow!" she cried, swatting Fuzzbutt away. "What? What's the matter?" She rubbed her hip. The mammoth had never literally dragged her out of bed before. Usually he just snuggled and poked her gently until she got up to let him out.

Captain Fuzzbutt tugged her to her feet and head-butted her toward the door.

"Okay, okay, I'm coming," she said. She shoved her feet into flip-flops and followed him down the stairs, rubbing her eyes. The clock in the kitchen said 7:22 a.m. Zoe yawned. "Why are you doing this to me, Captain?"

The mammoth let go of her and stormed into the living room, then back into the kitchen, then back into the living room.

Zoe followed him sleepily. She slid the glass door open, and Captain Fuzzbutt galloped out into the Menagerie.

Zoe squinted across the lawn. The rising sun was bright in her eyes, so it was hard to see at first, but it looked like someone was moving down on the shore of the lake.

Oh, it's just the kelpie, she realized, recognizing the gray water-horse. Then the kelpie moved to the side, and Zoe saw Logan standing right next to her. *Climbing onto her back.*

"Logan!" Zoe screamed.

It was too late. The kelpie dove into the water and sank instantly, taking Logan along with her.

Zoe flew down to the lake, shouting for help as she ran. Several curious mermaid faces popped out of the water. "Do something!" Zoe shouted. "The kelpie has Logan! Help him!"

The mermaids all made exaggerated gestures of "What? I can't hear you! I have absolutely no idea what you're saying!"

Captain Fuzzbutt was standing on the edge of the lake, trumpeting in panic. He was terrified of the water, but Zoe could tell he was almost ready to jump in. The last thing she needed was to rescue a drowning, thrashing mammoth, too.

"Get Blue!" she yelled, shoving the Captain toward the house. She ran into the water, losing her flip-flops instantly in the sucking sand, and dove at the spot where the kelpie had gone down.

The freezing water would have shocked her awake if her fear hadn't already. It was dark underwater, but she could see the shape of the kelpie sinking and Logan on her back, flailing desperately. Zoe was a good swimmer after years of training with Blue, so she caught up to them quickly.

But she had no idea how to separate a kelpie from her victim. She had never been properly kelpie-trained, since taking care of her was the mermaids' job. She grabbed Logan's hand, and he clutched hers like a lifeline. Zoe tried maneuvering around to brace her feet against the kelpie's side. She wrapped her arms around Logan's chest and shoved upward with all her might.

Nothing happened. This was magic; once a kelpie had you in the water, you were dead.

Not in my Menagerie, Zoe thought. She kicked the kelpie as hard as she could, but the horse didn't even react. Zoe was running out of air, and they were still sinking slowly through the dark water. She kept one arm around Logan and grabbed the kelpie's mane with the other hand, yanking hard.

The kelpie shook her head as if annoyed. Zoe yanked again, and the kelpie reared in the water, trying to shake Zoe off.

You're not getting rid of me unless you let go of Logan, Zoe thought fiercely. She glanced at Logan, who was swaying in a horribly unconscious way. *Stay alive. I'm not drowning for nothing.*

Something brushed against Zoe's back. She started,

nearly losing her grip on Logan. Was it the mermaids, coming to help at last?

A long purple tentacle snaked past Zoe and felt along the kelpie's neck. The kelpie shuddered and froze. Another tentacle slipped around Zoe from the other side and wound around Logan's waist.

The kraken. Zoe felt faint. *The kraken is awake.* They all thought she'd gone into hibernation a month ago.

She didn't dare move or turn around as more tentacles wove past her, winding around the kelpie and Logan and Zoe herself. The tentacles felt rubbery and prickly at the same time, like shark skin, and had small suction cups that stuck to Zoe's bare arms. Zoe gripped Logan's hand as tightly as she could. The lack of air was making her dizzy. Maybe she was even hallucinating all of this.

The kraken slid one tentacle around the kelpie's neck and slowly began to squeeze.

A stream of bubbles shot out of the kelpie's nose, and the water-horse began to kick and struggle with a horrible screaming sound that echoed through the water.

The kraken squeezed tighter.

Suddenly the kelpie gave an enormous kick, and Logan flew off her back. The kraken immediately flung the water-horse away and shot to the surface, towing Logan and Zoe in her tentacles.

Water rushed past Zoe so fast she felt like she was falling.

She burst out into the air, gasping and shivering. Beside her, Logan's eyes were closed, and his brown skin was frighteningly pale and clammy. She shook his hand. "Logan!"

The kraken gently deposited them on the lakeshore and let go. Zoe barely had time to see the tentacles slither back into the lake before a towel was wrapped around her shoulders and her father was picking her up in his strong arms. Logan's hand slid out of hers. She reached for it again, but Blue and Matthew and her mom were already there, wrapping towels around him and doing CPR.

Captain Fuzzbutt crowded into her dad, trying to dry Zoe with his trunk. Melissa was there, too, standing with her bare feet in the lake and yelling at Blue's dad.

"This is your fault!" she shouted. "You're supposed to watch the kelpie!"

"Why is there a man-child wandering the Menagerie at this hour?" Cobalt bellowed. He stood waist deep in the water, waving his arms in anger. "How were we supposed to know?"

"But you *did* know, and you didn't do *anything!*" Melissa shouted. "Do you know what would happen if someone died in here? You could be sent anywhere! They would do much worse than shut down the Menagerie—did you even think about that?"

Zoe felt cold, even with her father's hands rubbing her arms through the towel. She hadn't thought about what would happen to the Menagerie if the kelpie drowned

Logan. Her father turned toward the house, carrying her.

"Wait, Dad," she said, grabbing his shoulder. "Is Logan okay?"

As if he'd heard her, Logan suddenly coughed, then coughed again. Zoe's mom helped him sit up, and he spewed lake water all over the sand. Zoe leaned against her dad, feeling relief wash over her. Captain Fuzzbutt patted her head with his trunk.

"Dude," Matthew said. He sat back on his heels and wiped sweat off his forehead. "You scared the living daylights out of us."

"Didn't we tell you to stay away from the kelpie?" Blue said, shaking Logan's shoulder.

Logan took a few heaving, gasping breaths. "What's a kelpie?" he sputtered.

"Oh, brother." Matthew shook his head. "Maybe you were right, Zoe. Maybe he's better off not remembering this place."

"No, don't!" Logan grabbed Blue's arm and took another breath. "Don't wipe my memory. Please. I talked to Squorp. I think I know how to find the other cubs." He had another fit of coughing.

"Let's get you back to the house," said Zoe's mom. Matthew and Blue helped him stand up.

"I can walk, Dad," Zoe said. She gave him a hug as he put her down, and they all started slowly back up the hill.

Melissa stayed behind, still arguing with Cobalt.

"What happened?" Logan asked. Fuzzbutt squeezed in next to him so Logan could lean against his furry side as they walked. "I was drowning and then—I feel like I remember . . . pandas?"

Blue laughed, and Zoe felt herself turning bright red.

"Zoe's pajamas," Matthew said, pointing to the dripping legs of her pajama pants, which were covered in soccer-playing pandas. "She rescued you."

"I didn't do anything," Zoe said, embarrassed. "It was Captain Fuzzbutt and the kraken. Mostly the kraken." Her bare feet were freezing in the cold, dew-covered grass, but she didn't want to ask to be carried again.

"The kraken's awake?" said her mom. "That's odd."

"Thank you," Logan said to Zoe. "I guess I was an idiot."

"Well, yeah," she said.

"We could have warned you better," Matthew interjected. "Kelpies are kind of evil water-horses. That's like their whole thing—stand at the edge of a lake, look beautiful and wet, lure people into climbing on them. Then, *boom*, drowning. Usually followed by devouring. It's really not your fault you fell for it."

"I thought—" Logan stopped, glancing down at his feet. Zoe could guess what he was about to say. *I thought it liked me.* That's how the kelpie always made her feel, too. She just knew better than to go anywhere near it. Ever since she was four, Blue had been telling her all the mermaid horror stories about kelpies and their victims.

"Well, now you know," she said. "So don't worry about it."

"And the mermaids should have protected you, too, so they're in big trouble," said Zoe's dad. "I don't know what's gotten into them lately."

"With luck, Melissa will yell at Cobalt all day," Matthew joked. "That should make them *really* sorry. No offense, Blue."

Blue shrugged. "At least they're not fighting about me this time," he said.

Zoe's mom slid open the glass doors, and Captain Fuzzbutt practically shoved Zoe and Logan inside. Zoe's toes sank into the carpet, and she took a deep breath of the warm air.

"Cinnamon buns for breakfast," her dad said. "No arguments. I'll take care of it while you all shower and get dressed. Then we'll head out and find those last griffins. Right?" He tousled Zoe's wet hair.

"Right," Zoe said. She wished she could sound as confident as he did. After all, this wasn't exactly the best start to the day.

She watched Logan follow Blue up the stairs. As he got to the landing, he turned to look down, caught her eye, and smiled at her.

Then again, maybe everything wasn't so bad after all.

TWENTY-TWO

Logan studied the map of Xanadu laid out on the dining-room table. Zoe had insisted he have the first shower, so now she was upstairs while he and Blue had hot cocoa and cinnamon buns. His clothes had been whisked through the dryer again, but they still felt stiff and uncomfortable. He was trying really hard to act as casual as Blue, as if he wasn't still shaking on the inside.

"I totally get it now," Logan said to Blue.

"What's that?"

"Why Zoe's clothes are always a mess. I noticed it at school, and I figured she just didn't care about that stuff. But I've been here less than a day, and my clothes have been set on fire by a phoenix, drowned by a kelpie, rolled on by a mammoth, clawed and nibbled by griffin cubs, and drenched in kraken ink. It's amazing she has anything to wear to school at all."

"Well, it's also true she doesn't care about clothes," Blue said. He sat down in one of the squashy tan armchairs, holding his cocoa between his hands. "But I know what you mean. And you haven't even seen how much Zoe does around here. She's like a never-ending chore machine."

"Don't you have to do all that stuff, too?" Logan traced the streets from the Menagerie to his house with his finger on the map.

"Not exactly," Blue said, sounding a little guilty. "I'm— it's kind of a whole thing with my dad."

"Was that your dad down at the lake?" The shouting green-bearded man had looked familiar from the photo in Blue's room.

"Yeah." Blue shifted uncomfortably and then muttered into his cocoa. "He'skindoftheking."

Logan pivoted to look at him. Blue shook his hair forward into his face and avoided Logan's eyes.

"Hang on," Logan said. "Did you just say your dad is a *king?*"

"That's right," Matthew said, swinging into the room from the kitchen. He grabbed four cinnamon buns off the plate on the table. "King of the mermaids, at least the ones living here. Which makes Blue, obviously, a prince."

Blue winced. "It's no big deal," he said. "But Dad doesn't like it when he catches me doing chores, that's all. I'm supposed to help with mermaid stuff, but he doesn't let me do much of that, either."

"Tough life," Logan joked.

"Well," Matthew said with his mouth full, "keep in mind that Melissa is his mom."

"Hey," Blue said mildly. "Shut up."

"I'm just saying, he might not have to do chores, but he does have to be in the most advanced math class and get straight As or Melissa will flip. So that's not fun, exactly," Matthew said. "Right, Blue?"

Blue shrugged. "It's fine."

Mr. Kahn came into the room clapping his hands and rubbing them together. "All right, Logan," he said. "Let's see your Tracker instincts at work."

Matthew gave him an odd look—part curious, part offended, Logan thought. But Mr. Kahn went on without noticing. "Where do you think we should start looking for the griffins?" He leaned over the map on the table.

Logan sat down nearby. He liked the way Mr. Kahn treated him like another grown-up. It made up, a little, for how incredibly stupid he felt about the kelpie.

"Here's what I know," he said, pulling a notepad and pen toward him. "There's a red male who really likes food. I bet he's the one who ate everything in the school cafeteria."

"Definitely," Zoe said from the doorway. She was wearing a dark blue turtleneck, jeans, and small silver earrings. Her hair was still wet, and she was rubbing it with a white towel. She actually didn't look like a total mess for once.

As she sat down next to him, Logan realized her earrings were tiny silver griffins. "Cool," he said. "I like your earrings."

She touched her ears. "For luck," she said.

He slid the plate of cinnamon buns over to her and she took one.

Mr. Kahn was nodding, staring at the map. "So we look for anywhere with a lot of food missing. Good idea."

"Maybe the pizza place," Logan said, tapping the restaurant near the library. "I noticed it was closed last night, which is weird."

"What about the other two griffins?" Zoe asked.

"I don't have any ideas for the gray female yet," Logan said. "Squorp told me she likes secrets and she's clever. Not much to work with. But the other one, the brown male, his name is Clonk. He wants to be just like Clink, so I think he'll be trying to follow in her footsteps."

"Figures," Matthew snorted. "Bossy older sisters. Zoe and I know all about that. Luckily her big brother is totally awesome." He tapped the chore wheel by the doors. "For instance, I did your Aviary rounds last night, so you can pick up mine today while I'm out with Mom and Dad searching for griffins."

Zoe rolled her eyes. "Fine. I'll add it to my list." She pulled out her notebook with all the triangles and squiggles; Logan realized it must be a kind of code. Each item had a little box in front of it, some checked off, most of them not. She muttered to herself as she wrote. "Feed the salamanders, ask Mooncrusher for an extra blanket for Pelly, Saturday fire safety equipment check, let Captain graze by the griffin enclosure before that grass gets too long, check on Scratch in case he's not eating because he's sick—"

"Actually, Zoe," said her dad. "You're on griffin-hunting duty today and that's it."

"Wait, what?" Matthew looked startled. "Zoe's coming with us?"

"You're not going anywhere," Mr. Kahn corrected. "I need you to install the software updates on SNAPA's list."

Matthew crossed his arms. "But *I'm* the one with Tracker training. *I* should be looking for the griffins."

"You're also the only one who can wrestle that computer, which is why I asked you to install the updates earlier this week. I don't know what you've been doing instead, but now they have to get done. So you're staying here until it's finished."

"I think my training—"

"Training isn't everything," said Mr. Kahn. He winked at Logan. "Instincts count for a lot, too."

Matthew frowned and turned to look out at the Menagerie. "Who's going to do the chores?" he asked.

"Keiko will do them for you and Zoe."

Matthew let out a slightly strangled noise, and Zoe raised her eyebrows. "Oh, really?" she said. "Which Keiko is that? Not the one who lives here."

"We'll take care of it," her dad said firmly. "I have to go speak with Cobalt about the grate and the kelpie. Zoe, I want you and Logan and Blue to head out now and start looking for Clonk. Trust Logan's instincts and your smarts. Your mom and I will go out looking for the red cub as soon as we can. Matthew, if you're done with the computer by then, you can come with us." He smiled at Logan. "We'll start at the pizza place."

Matthew snorted and stalked off to Melissa's office without looking at any of them. Logan felt vaguely guilty, as if he'd caused a fight—but surely the same thing would have happened with or without him there. He hoped Matthew wasn't mad at him.

He checked his phone while Zoe and Blue got their bikes, but there were no messages from his dad. He probably thought it was way too early for Logan to be up on a Saturday. Logan sent him a text that said **Thanx for letting me stay over last night. Going biking w Blue now.**

A minute later his phone buzzed. **Sounds great. Have fun.**

They paused at the bottom of the driveway, and Logan saw Zoe looking up the street toward the Sterling mansion. She twisted one hand around the other wrist and turned to him. "We saw brown feathers outside the post office yesterday. But Matthew managed to check inside while we were in school and said he didn't find anything."

"I get it," Logan said. "The post office has those steps and columns outside. To Clonk it would kind of look like the bank, where Clink went. Let's check it again."

The post office and school were in the center of town, halfway between the Menagerie and Logan's house. The school, of course, was deserted on a Saturday. It looked kind of weirdly abandoned, like in a zombie movie.

To Logan's disappointment, the post office wasn't open yet. He poked the sign on the door. "Ten to noon?" he said. "Jeez, maybe I should be a postal worker when I grow up."

"The feathers are gone," Zoe said, scanning the steps.

"Probably blew away," Blue said.

Logan glanced across the street and saw someone drive into the school parking lot. Instinct made him grab Zoe and Blue and pull them behind one of the columns.

"Look," he said, nodding at the lot.

It was the school librarian again—Miss Sameera. She parked her white Vespa and stood on the front steps of the school for a moment, looking up and down the street and twirling something in her hands.

Suddenly Zoe gasped and grabbed Logan's arm. "Look!" she whispered.

The librarian was holding a large brown feather.

TWENTY-THREE

Miss Sameera bounced up the school steps. Today her long skirt was bright purple, with little bells along the bottom, and her tunic top was covered in large yellow sunflowers. She didn't *look* particularly sinister, Logan thought.

"What do we do?" Zoe whispered as the librarian disappeared into the school. "Do you think she knows something?"

"Well," Logan said, "she has been acting a little . . . weird." He told them about the conversation he'd had with her outside the cafeteria. And about the mythical-creature books she'd been checking out of the library.

"Huh," said Blue. "I thought she was nice."

"She *is* nice," Zoe said, worry wrinkles crinkling between her eyebrows. "But we should follow her."

They ran down the post office steps and across the empty street to the school. The school library was on the ground floor, in a wing of its own at the back. The three of them ran around the outside of the school to the library windows, which were big and wide and usually open a crack because the heat was on too high.

Logan crouched beside a window and peeked in, then quickly ducked down again. Miss Sameera was at her desk, typing at her computer.

"Maybe she's not up to anything," he whispered. "Maybe she's just here to work."

A cell phone began to buzz.

"Hello?" Miss Sameera said. "Oh, Mr. Claverhill! Thank you for calling me back. Sir, I was right about Xanadu." She paused, then said in an injured voice, "No, I know you're still not paying for my trip. But listen. This town is crawling with mythical creatures."

Zoe gasped, and Blue clapped one hand over her mouth.

"Well, I don't know yet," said the librarian. "But I've seen two so far. Griffin cubs. I'm serious! Yes, I'm sure!" She paused. "This is completely different. I'm not— Now, listen, I chased a brown one from the post office into town yesterday, but I lost him in the park. And then I spotted a gray one early this morning, up in the hills where the mansions are."

Logan saw tears starting in Zoe's eyes. He took one of her hands and squeezed it.

"Sir," Miss Sameera said with icy politeness, "I think I know the difference between a coyote and a griffin cub." She paused. "Well, you don't have to believe me. I followed that Tracker here, and now I know I was right. And you'll believe it, too, when I come riding back to headquarters on a unicorn!" They heard the librarian fling her phone down on the desk. "They'll all see," she muttered, tapping something on her keyboard.

"Come on," Logan whispered. They ran back to their bikes, staying low and close to the wall so Miss Sameera wouldn't see them.

"What if she has pictures?" Zoe burst out as soon as they were out of earshot. "What if she's blogging about the cubs right now? What if SNAPA sees it? What if exterminators are already looking for them?"

"If she had photos, she'd have sent them to the guy on the phone," Logan pointed out.

"And she's not blogging," Blue said calmly. "She hates the internet. I used Wikipedia for our last research assignment, and she gave me a whole lecture about not trusting what you read online."

"We should tell Dad," Zoe said, twisting her hand around her wrist. "Shouldn't we?"

"No," Blue said. "Find the cubs first. Before she does. That's priority one."

"The park," Logan said. He clipped on his bike helmet. "At least we have a lead."

They biked toward the center of town. "What if she knows about the Menagerie?" Zoe said at the next stoplight. "What if she's the one who snuck in and unbolted the gate?"

"The intruder alert would have gone off," Blue said.

"And then she'd know about a lot more than two cubs," Logan pointed out.

"Maybe she was lying to the guy on the phone. And she did mention unicorns," Zoe said.

Logan couldn't think of anything reassuring to say.

The park was only a few blocks wide, with a fenced-in dog run on one end and several red wooden benches under the large, shady trees. Most of Xanadu's little shops were clustered in the square around it, including the bookstore, a consignment shop, a toy store, the pharmacy, a candy store, a sandwich shop, and a pet store.

Blue and Zoe each found a large stick and started gently poking the bushes. Logan climbed onto the base of the stone statue in the middle and surveyed the shops.

If he were a griffin on the run, where would he go?

He imagined being Clonk—driven away by his sister when all he wanted was to follow her around. Where would Clonk go to prove he could find treasure just as well as Clink could?

His gaze landed on one of the store displays and he smiled.

"Zoe," he called, hopping down from the statue. "I'm going to check in there." He pointed at the toy store. The entire window was filled with a pirate-themed display, including a Lego pirate ship, pirate hats and capes and eye patches for Halloween costumes, and stuffed parrots perched on fake trees. And most importantly, chests overflowing with gold coins and plastic jewels.

"Then I'm coming with you," Zoe said. "Since you're always right about everything."

"It's just a guess," Logan said. He didn't explain that searching for griffins was the first thing he'd been good at in a long time. He was too afraid of messing it up, especially after his mistake with the kelpie.

They left Blue checking the trees and crossed the street to the toy store. A hand was just flipping the sign to OPEN; Logan checked his watch and saw that it was a little after nine o'clock. Giant signs in the window advertised trick-or-treating on Halloween night, with ten percent off everything in the store all day for anyone in a pirate costume.

A bell jingled above their heads as Zoe pulled the door open. *Jackpot,* Logan thought. The store was crammed wall-to-wall with toys, overflowing and piled all over each other. A giant tree at the back had stuffed animals stuck in all the branches and climbing the trunk, making it look like a furry pink-and-purple volcano. A model train ran on a track near the ceiling, *click-clack*ing around and around. One corner of the store had been taken over by racks of Halloween costumes and a wall of masks. Board books and board games were stacked on shelves and pouring out of trunks. Baby rattles and toy trucks and tambourines were scattered across the Sesame Street carpet, where kids could play with them while their parents shopped.

It would not be hard to hide something the size of a puppy in here.

Behind the counter, a grandfatherly old man in a wheelchair looked up and beamed at them. He wore a pirate skull-and-crossbones hat rakishly tilted on his bald head. "Looking for costumes, my dears?" he asked. "You both look like you'd make excellent pirates. *Arrr!*"

"No, thanks," Zoe said. "We're just browsing for a present. For, uh, my sister."

Logan was glad she didn't point out that they were too old for trick-or-treating. He didn't want to hurt the feelings of the nice old guy with the pirate obsession.

"Let me know if I can help," the man said, still beaming. "I'm full of suggestions."

Logan squeezed past Zoe and checked the rack of costumes. Several of the robes and capes reached to the floor, and he thought a griffin cub might be able to hide behind them. But there was nothing under or behind the rack.

Zoe was casually trying to prod the pirate display in the window without knocking it all over. Logan turned and studied the tree. It had nooks and crannies all over it, most of them crammed with stuffed animals. He checked the branches, moving surly-looking flamingoes and monkey puppets with long tails. Nothing.

He edged closer and started carefully searching the mound of toys. There were an awful lot of stuffed polar bears in every possible size. Also panda bears. Not many birds except for penguins. He saw only one big eagle buried at the back.

And then the eagle blinked.

TWENTY-FOUR

Zoe ran her fingers through the gold coins in the chest, checked that the manager wasn't watching, and then stuck her arm into the trunk full of pirate booty. It was a long shot, but maybe there was a griffin cub buried under all this. . . .

"Hey, Zoe," Logan said. "Check it out. I bet Keiko would like this."

For a moment Zoe thought he was serious and wondered why on earth she would get Keiko anything. Then she turned and saw him making incredibly obvious faces at the pile of stuffed animals.

Of course he found the cub, she thought. *He's an even*

better natural Tracker than Matthew. Not that that bothered her or anything.

She strolled back to where he was and saw the griffin's head sticking out of a sea of fuzzy dogs and adorable tigers.

"It's okay," Logan said to the cub in a low voice. "We'll get you out of here."

The griffin blinked at him.

"He says he's the greatest pirate in the world, and he's not leaving without his treasure," Logan reported. "What treasure, Clonk?"

The griffin shuffled a bit to the side. Underneath his paws was a wild nest of Monopoly money and fake pirate gold coins.

"He says he'd have more if the pirate behind the desk hadn't been watching that window treasure like a hawk all day yesterday. I guess he slept through the hours when the store was closed."

"This one does sleep a lot," Zoe whispered. The cub clacked his beak at her.

"Clonk wants to know whether anyone else has found as much glorious treasure as he has," Logan said. "Clonk, I think it's safe to say no one found anything like this. Your brothers and sisters will be so impressed when you get home and tell them."

The griffin ruffled his feathers in a pleased way.

"How do we get him out of here?" Logan asked. He paused. "With all his glorious treasure, yes."

Zoe glanced around the store. She had the sling in her backpack, but that worked best at night; it would be a lot more obvious riding through Xanadu like that in the middle of the day.

Her eyes landed on a display of Fancy Nancy accessories. In the middle of it was a glittering pink backpack, practically bursting with sequins.

"I am going to regret this," Zoe said, picking up the backpack. It would be a squeeze, but Clonk was nearly the smallest griffin, no bigger than a collie puppy. "Distract him," she whispered, nodding at the storekeeper.

"I'll buy your treasure so we can take it with us," Logan said to Clonk. There was a pause, and he added, "I know, pirates don't have to buy their treasure. But would you really steal from a fellow pirate?" He motioned at the storekeeper. "Where is your pirate honor, Clonk?"

The griffin cub drew himself up proudly and then moved aside so Logan could gather all the gold coins. Zoe found a small leather bag, and Logan took everything up to the counter to pay for it.

While the storekeeper was focused on Logan, Zoe unzipped the backpack and helped Clonk climb inside. He clacked his beak and made grumbling sounds and rearranged his tail and wings about a thousand times, but finally she zipped the pink sparkles around him and carried the bag up to the counter.

"Lovely," the storekeeper said, beaming some more as he handed Logan his change. "If your sister can't be a pirate, Fancy Nancy is an excellent alternative." Zoe kept a tight hold on the bag while he rang up the price. She didn't want him to pick it up and notice how heavy it was. She felt like a total shoplifter, until she saw the price of the backpack.

"Forty dollars!" she whispered to Logan, slinging the bag over her back. "Now I feel like *I* just got shoplifted from." She hoped her parents would pay her back. That was a lot of allowance gone at once.

"Just think about how sparkly and pretty you look," he teased. "And so very, very fancy." He held the door open for her and pretended to bow.

"Merci," she joked.

They stepped out onto the sidewalk and ran right into Jasmin Sterling and her brother, Jonathan, coming out of the pharmacy.

Of course. *Of course* Jasmin would see her like this.

Jasmin spotted the Fancy Nancy backpack right away. Her eyebrows arched so high Zoe thought the top of her head might fly off.

When they were six years old, Zoe and Jasmin had had Fancy Nancy sleepovers once a month. Always at Jasmin's house, of course; Jasmin was allergic to cats, so Zoe's family pretended they had seven of them so Jasmin could never come over. Neither Jasmin nor Zoe minded. Jasmin's house was enormous, and she had all the best toys, including every Fancy Nancy accessory in the universe.

Zoe had always slept better at Jasmin's house than anywhere else, with her best friend curled up beside her, no Menagerie chores waiting for her in the morning, and no mythical creatures howling or squawking outside her window. She remembered lying in Jasmin's Fancy Nancy sleeping bag, wishing she could switch places and just *be* Jasmin.

"What—what—" Jasmin's eyes shot to Logan, who was standing close behind Zoe. Jasmin looked like she was having some kind of apoplectic fit where she couldn't decide what to make fun of first.

"Hi, Zoe," Jonathan said. He was taller than she remembered from the high school graduation ceremony in June, where he'd been elected to give the class speech. His blue-black hair was longer, curling just below his ears and slicked to one side of his face. He still had the nose stud he and Ruby had gotten at the same time last Christmas, although his was a tiny diamond. He also still had the vaguely confused look he'd started wearing after Ruby wiped his memories.

"How's your sister?" he asked, taking the pharmacy bag from Jasmin and tucking it into his messenger bag.

"Great," Zoe said awkwardly. She knew he didn't remember anything about his relationship with Ruby—it was too interwoven with the Menagerie secrets they'd erased. But her parents said he'd probably still feel attracted to Ruby whenever they were together, which was why everyone made sure they were never, ever together.

"Who are you?" Jasmin blurted at Logan.

"Seriously? He's in our class, Jasmin," Zoe said. She was pretty sure Jasmin just wanted to make a point about how much of a nobody he was. As if anyone who wanted to be friends with Zoe was beneath her notice.

"Logan Wilde." Logan held out his hand, and Jasmin eyed it like he was handing her a dying piranha.

"Well, see you around," Zoe said, backing toward the street.

"Ooh la *la*," Jasmin said, imitating Fancy Nancy's catchphrase. Apparently she'd recovered from her shock. "Hurrying off with Logan for a private *rendezvous?*"

Zoe knew she was turning red again. She glanced at Jonathan, but his vague, faraway look told her he wasn't going to be any help with his sister.

Unexpectedly, Logan put his arm around Zoe's shoulder. "Yup, you figured us out. Sorry, we have to go."

Jasmin's mouth fell open. Logan grabbed Zoe's hand, and they sprinted across the street to the park. They didn't stop until they reached the dog run on the far side, where an old Pekingese was waddling slowly from fence post to fence post while a Great Dane tried to play with it.

Zoe wrenched her hand out of Logan's. "What the heck was that?" she demanded.

"Sorry," he said, spreading his palms. "I had to distract her and cover up the backpack before she noticed it was moving. Clonk, stop trying to unzip it!" Zoe felt furious wriggling under the fabric, and a beak poked her grumpily in the back.

"Ow," she said. She set the backpack on the ground and rubbed her head with both hands. "Well, I guess if she wants to make fun of us, she'll have to acknowledge I exist first."

Logan looked at her curiously. "Do you care? She doesn't seem like your kind of person."

"She used to be," Zoe said. "She was my best friend until about five months ago. But I had to stop being friends with her after her brother and my sister broke up. It was . . . bad."

"That doesn't seem fair." Logan leaned over the fence so the Great Dane could sniff his hand. The dog licked his fingers, and Logan scratched behind his floppy ears. Did every animal on the planet immediately fall in love with this guy? Apart from the kelpie, of course.

"Jonathan's the reason we never let strangers leave the Menagerie without a memory wipe, no matter who it is," Zoe said with a sigh. "Ruby was sure we could trust him. They dated for almost a year, and he got to know pretty much everything about the Menagerie. If we'd given him kraken ink every night, he'd have forgotten the creatures and remembered Ruby. But by the time we figured out what he was up to, the kraken ink dosage had to be so high it basically wiped their whole relationship from his brain."

Logan stared at the Great Dane, his hand moving slowly through the black fur. "So—what does he remember?"

"We don't know for sure." Zoe rubbed her wrist. "Ruby had to give his parents some, too, since we weren't sure if he'd told them about the Menagerie."

"And Jasmin?"

Zoe shook her head. "I could tell she didn't know anything, but they made me give her the kraken ink anyway." She took a deep breath. That had been one of the worst days of her life. "I was right, though—there were no supernatural memories to erase." Which actually made it harder, since Jasmin remembered everything about their friendship and had no idea why Zoe had suddenly ditched her.

"So why couldn't you stay friends?" Logan asked.

"Too risky." Zoe glanced back at the store, but Jasmin was gone. "Everyone was worried that any extended contact with the Sterlings might bring back their memories. Brain wiping isn't an exact science. If, like, I was sleeping over at Jasmin's and Jonathan talked to me for too long, he might start having flashbacks. We just have to keep the Sterlings as far away from us as possible from now on, basically."

"Oh," Logan said. He thought for a moment. "Still doesn't seem fair."

Zoe agreed with him. Ruby always said Zoe's sacrifice was nothing compared to hers. But Zoe figured seven years of best friendship was at least as important as a year of "absolute true love forever," especially with a rotten creep like Jonathan.

Blue dropped out of a tree just across the park, almost giving the Pekingese a heart attack. The two dogs in the run barked indignantly at him as he trotted around to Zoe and Logan.

"No luck?" he asked. Then he tripped over the sparkly backpack, which squawked at him.

"Lots of luck," Zoe said, nudging the backpack with her toe. "Except I really do not want to ride home wearing this."

"I'll do it," Blue said without hesitating. He picked up the backpack and put it on. "How about I run this guy home, and you keep looking for the next one?"

"Sure," Logan said. "And maybe we could stop by my house, too, if that's okay. I'd like to feed my pets and change."

"Great. I'll catch up with you soon." Blue hopped on his bike and pedaled off, pink sequins sparkling cheerfully on his back. He didn't look even a little bit embarrassed.

Logan's expression, watching him go, said *I will never be that cool.* Which Zoe thought was kind of ridiculous; anyone willing to stand up to Jasmin Sterling or put out a burning phoenix didn't have a problem with bravery, and that seemed cool enough to her.

"All right," she said. "Let's look for the red one next."

"The one who loves food," Logan said, nodding. "That should make tracking him pretty simple. I bet this is the easiest one of all."

TWENTY-FIVE

Six hours later, Logan sat down on the bench outside the ice-cream shop and rubbed his sore legs.

"I cursed us," he said ruefully. "Why is there so much food in this town?"

"You mean, why *was* there," Zoe said. She pulled out her phone and started typing a message to her parents.

"School cafeteria," Logan said, counting on his fingers. "Pizza place. Candy store. The Dumpster behind the supermarket. The Dumpster behind the sandwich shop. All the cat food in the pet store, but none of the dog food. We're lucky he didn't try to break into the hamster cages. The freezers at both Chinese food places and the Mexican place.

All the Twinkies in the 7-Eleven, but nothing else, so maybe he's finally getting full."

"It's like we're searching for a bottomless pit instead of a griffin cub," Zoe said. Her phone buzzed. "Okay, Mom and Dad are at the Buffalo Bill Diner, but everything seems normal there. And Blue is still stuck in crisis management with his parents. I guess the mermaids haven't done all the underwater things on SNAPA's list yet." She sighed. "I feel like I should be there helping. I'm better at the scuba work than Matthew is."

"You are helping," Logan said. "Finding the cubs is the most important thing, right?"

"Maybe I'd feel that way if we *were* finding a cub," she said ruefully.

"Well, let's think," Logan said. "This cub is fast, stealthy, and on a totally different mission than the others."

"Mission Eat the Entire Planet Before We Stop Him," Zoe agreed.

Logan stood and began pacing up and down the sidewalk. They hadn't made it to his house yet, and he was starting to fantasize longingly about clean T-shirts. They also hadn't stopped for lunch, although it didn't seem like the red griffin had left anything uneaten in the whole town anyway.

A few blocks down the street, a flash of reflected light from one of the library windows caught Logan's eye. "Hey," he said, "there was a flyer in the library about missing sheep.

Is there any chance the griffin could have eaten those, too?"

Zoe shoved back her hair and twisted one of her earrings as she thought. "I doubt it," she said. "Even after eating all this, he'd still be smaller than a sheep, and the cubs have never learned to hunt or kill anything. Besides, that flyer's probably been up for a while. The ranchers around here are always complaining about something."

"Okay." Logan stopped and rocked back on his heels. "Think. What does this griffin like to eat more than anything else? Does he have a favorite food?" He scratched his arms. "Can we think and bike to my house at the same time?"

Zoe nodded and followed him to their bikes. The morning chill had burned off quickly and it seemed like a hotter day than normal for late October. Logan led the way to his house, cutting through the supermarket parking lot on the way. He glanced at the Dumpsters again. From the mess and the way the bags were piled like a nest, he was afraid the griffin had slept there, which meant he was not going to be very pleasant smelling once they found him.

For the first time that day, Logan started feeling weird as he unlocked his door and let Zoe inside. While they were out searching, he hadn't even thought about how he was hanging out alone with a girl. But now she was in his house, and it was Zoe Kahn, of all people. Not the first friend he'd expected to bring home, and possibly the last girl.

He glanced around his living room and wished he'd vacuumed the beige carpet last week the way his dad had asked him to. It seemed like he could see crumbs everywhere. His Gatorade was still on the coffee table from yesterday afternoon. And Purrsimmon was sitting on top of the brown leather armchair, glaring at him. *Replace ME with a griffin cub?* her expression said. *WELL, I NEVER.*

"Sorry, Purrs," Logan said, offering her his hand. She turned up her nose at him and twitched her tail.

"I'll just be a minute," Logan said to Zoe. He took the mouse food he'd bought at the pet store into his room, closed the door, and fed Mr. and Mrs. Smith, who looked a lot happier now that a griffin wasn't eyeing them hungrily through the glass. Logan shoveled his clothes off the floor into the laundry basket. As he dug through his drawers, Zoe started talking to him through the door.

"The griffins all like fish," she said. "We have a lot of fish in the lake, so the griffins get plenty of that. Um. Matthew gave them chocolate once, and they all freaked out—it was like a griffin rodeo in there for the rest of the day." Her voice wandered away, as if she was exploring his living room.

Logan grabbed an orange T-shirt with a bulldog on it, gave it a quick sniff, and then discarded it again. *There's got to be something clean in here somewhere.* He finally found a striped yellow-and-gray T-shirt and switched out his cargo pants for blue jeans, plus a gray zippered hoodie.

"We grilled for the whole Menagerie for the Fourth of July." Zoe's voice sounded like she was in the kitchen now. "The cubs were only a month old at that point, but they each got a cheeseburger. They totally loved—" She stopped talking abruptly.

"Zoe?" Logan called. She didn't answer. *Uh-oh*, Logan thought. What could she have found? Was there anything embarrassing in the kitchen?

He threw on new socks and different sneakers, poured fish food into Warrior's bowl, and ran back through the living room.

Zoe was standing in front of the refrigerator, staring at the door.

"What?" Logan asked. "Did you think of something the griffin would want?"

"Um—yeah," Zoe said. "Yes. Cheeseburgers. Right. I have to call my dad. Stay here."

Logan blinked as she disappeared out the front door. What the heck? He glanced at the fridge. It was covered in magnets from Chicago, old photos, invitations to his dad's department events, recycling info, a calendar, and a couple of takeout menus. Nothing very dramatic here.

Unless she'd noticed the department of wildlife heading on his dad's papers. Logan rubbed his head, worrying. Yes, his dad's department would probably want to know about griffins and dragons in their neighborhood. But surely Zoe knew he would never *tell* his dad about the Menagerie.

Maybe she was mad that he hadn't mentioned his dad's job. Mad enough to wipe his memories? Would she think he was a threat to the Menagerie now? Would Blue agree with her?

Logan got a couple of clear plastic bottles and filled them with water, to make sure he'd have something safe to drink, just in case. He also wrote a quick note to his dad, letting him know he'd been home. Then, since Zoe still wasn't back, he made them both peanut butter sandwiches with blueberry jam. He packed up some carrot sticks and a couple of oatmeal raisin cookies. They could take everything to go and keep searching.

He gave the door a nervous look. This seemed like a long conversation. *Focus on the griffins. The more useful you are, the more likely they are to trust you and keep you around.*

"Cheeseburgers," he muttered. Squorp had eaten a fair amount of their hamburger meat, but he found another block of it at the back of the freezer and defrosted it in the microwave. He separated out two patties and cooked them on their countertop grill, then packed the rest of the meat into a cooler bag with several slices of American cheese and a squeeze bottle of ketchup. Just in case, he threw in a bottle of chocolate syrup as well, then packed a few other supplies in his backpack.

He was just zipping up the bag when Zoe opened the front door. She definitely looked upset.

"What happened?" Logan asked. "Is everything okay?"

Zoe nodded, but the look on her face was the same as the one he'd seen Friday morning when she was lying to him about losing her dog. Logan wondered if he should bring up his dad's job . . . but if that wasn't the problem, he didn't want to *make* it the problem.

"I made sandwiches," Logan said, pushing hers toward her. "And I have an idea about the cheeseburgers."

"Okay," Zoe said. "Whatever you think. Let's just go."

Logan hesitated. *Maybe she'll be willing to talk about it after we find the next griffin,* he thought. "Bye, Purrsimmon," he called into the living room. "I promise you're still my favorite cat."

"*RRRREOW,*" she grumbled.

Outside, Logan stared at his bike for a moment, holding the two cooked hamburgers in a napkin in his hand.

"What's happening?" Zoe asked.

"I was thinking we'd ride through town with these and lure him to the grills in Teddy Roosevelt Park," Logan said. "But I can't figure out how to attach a hamburger to my bicycle."

Zoe covered her mouth with one hand, like she was fighting back a laugh. "Let me see."

Finally Logan went back inside for some dental floss,

which they used to tie one of the hamburgers to the book rack on the back of his bike. It was kind of gross, even with a paper towel underneath it, since the meat was still a bit raw and drippy.

"My poor bike," Logan said.

"I just hope Jasmin doesn't see me like this," Zoe said. Her bike didn't have a book rack, so they tied the other hamburger onto the front like a meaty headlamp. "It's a level of weird I don't think I've ever reached before."

Logan laughed. "All right, so I'll go one way through town and you go the other way, and hopefully the griffin will catch the scent and follow us there."

"See you at the reserve," Zoe said, wheeling her bike down the drive. She hesitated at the bottom, looked back at him like she wanted to say something, then took off.

That summer, whenever Logan's dad wasn't working on a weekend, he'd taken Logan to his favorite wildlife preserve: Teddy Roosevelt Park, right on the outskirts of Xanadu. There were hiking trails and fishing ponds, but most importantly, at least for what Logan wanted, there was an open grassy picnic area with tables and grills.

He got there a few moments before Zoe and picked a grill not far from the trees. "We're supposed to have a permit to use this," Logan said as she came up. He winced, realizing how "department of wildlife" that sounded.

"It's nearly November," Zoe pointed out. "I'm sure no one

really cares. I'll text my parents to meet us here."

Logan pulled a small bag of charcoal out of his backpack and tipped it into the grill. He was about to light a match when a family came out of the woods nearby, and he had to quickly hide the matchbook in his hand.

Besides the parents, there were three guys and two little girls. He recognized one of the guys from school—Marco Jimenez, soccer captain and class clown, and one of the only other different-looking faces in the seventh grade. Marco squinted at Zoe and Logan across the field while his family climbed into their minivan. It occurred to Logan that this might look really weird, hanging around a grill with Zoe, alone, at this time of year. He smiled and waved, hoping that was the normal-person thing to do.

To his surprise, Marco waved back. A few minutes later, they were gone, and Logan lit the grill.

"Everyone's coming," Zoe said, pocketing her phone. He wasn't sure she'd even noticed Marco.

"Hopefully the red griffin will, too, once he smells this," Logan said.

Logan put the first uncooked hamburger patty on the grill, and they sat down at the picnic table to eat their sandwiches. Zoe kept glancing at him with that same look, like she wanted to say something, but whenever he met her eyes, she'd turn away again.

"You know what?" he said finally. "You should hide. He

doesn't know who I am, but if the griffin sees you, he might know it's a trap." *Also, it would be great to not sit here in awkward silence.*

Zoe ran her hands through her hair and nodded. "Okay. Good idea." She threw her leftovers in the trash and ran her bike over to the restrooms shack next to the parking lot.

The first hamburger turned into a charred lump, and Logan threw it out, putting another one on in its place. He added a piece of cheese in case that helped.

Nothing happened for what seemed like a long time. Logan ate a few carrot sticks and checked his watch. Maybe this wasn't going to work after all.

Just then he felt a prickling sensation along his spine. He knew what that feeling meant.

Someone was watching him.

TWENTY-SIX

Logan leaned on the table casually, searching the trees out of the corner of his eye. It took him a moment to spot it: a few yards away, hidden in the red and orange leaves of a tall oak tree, a pair of sharp black eyes was peering at the smoking grill.

Whistling, Logan added a few more hamburgers to the grill. He'd forgotten to bring a plate, so he slid the cooked cheeseburger onto his paper sandwich bag.

"Mmmm," he said loudly. "I'll just let this cool off for a minute." He set the cheeseburger on the end of the table closest to the woods, then bent down to get a water bottle out of his bag.

When he sat up again, the cheeseburger was gone.

Okay, THAT was fast, Logan thought. He'd expected to catch the griffin midtheft, but the cub must have flashed in and out of the trees at warp speed.

"Huh," he said out loud. "Did I eat that and forget about it? Weird!" The new hamburgers weren't cooked through yet, but he was sure the griffin cub wouldn't care. He put another one out on the bag and glanced in the direction Zoe had vanished. What were they supposed to do now?

"SQUOOORP."

Logan jumped. That sounded closer than the trees. He looked around slowly, then crouched.

The griffin cub was hiding under a picnic table a few feet away.

His feathers and fur were a warm, rusty red tinged with orange around the wingtips. He looked uncomfortably squished under the table, and Logan could tell he was quite a bit bigger than Squorp and Clonk—not as tall as Clink, but much rounder. This griffin definitely would not have fit in a backpack. Crumbs and bits of food were stuck to his chest feathers and big lion paws.

He stared at Logan solemnly.

"Oh, hey," Logan said. "Do you like hamburgers? I have a couple more."

The griffin gave him a wide-eyed, plaintive look, as if he hadn't eaten in weeks.

"With cheese?" Logan offered.

Cheeeeese, the griffin agreed, clacking his beak. Logan beckoned, holding out the burger, and the griffin cub wriggled squashily out from under the table. He edged closer to Logan, eyeing the cheeseburger, but stopped warily out of reach.

"Do you have a name yet?" Logan asked. He sat down on the grass and opened one of the cheese slices for himself.

The griffin shook his head.

"Maybe we should call you . . ." Logan thought about the griffin's brothers and sisters. Clink, Clonk, Squorp, Flurp. "Hmm. How about Yump?"

Yump, the griffin thought. **Yump. Yump hungry. Yump like food. Yump want meat. Yump Yump Yump. Does sound like me.** He flicked his tail across the grass and gave Logan an eagle smile. **Better than Roly-Poly. YUMP.**

"Great," Logan said. Poor Zoe and her hopelessly wrong names for the cubs. "Have a cheeseburger, Yump."

The griffin cub stretched his neck forward and snatched the burger out of Logan's hands. He backed up a few steps and gobbled it down.

"So, Yump," Logan said. "Do you miss your family?"

Yump made a sound like a snort. **Not one bit.** He stretched his wings expressively. **No sharing out here! Best world ever!**

"Okay," Logan said. So that strategy wasn't going to work. "What's your favorite thing you've eaten today?"

Cheeseburgers, Yump thought at once. **No, pizza. No, frozen dumplings. No, Twinkies. Wait! Yummy cans of cat. No . . . cheeseburgers.**

"Please don't tell me you thought you were actually eating cat," Logan said.

Yump tilted his head at him. **Pictures of cats on cans!**

"Terrible, Yump," Logan said. "That was food FOR cats. You shouldn't eat cats anyway. You're, like, distantly related." Purrsimmon had enough problems without having to dodge hungry griffin cubs when she went out at night.

Hmmm, the griffin said, sidling closer. **More cheeseburgers?**

Logan got up and slid the last burgers off the grill. He set them down on the table next to him and held out his hand. Yump delicately placed his front paw in Logan's palm and allowed Logan to help him waddle up onto the table.

"You know," Logan said, "I heard the Menagerie was thinking of making every Friday Cheeseburger Night."

The griffin's head shot up, and he stared at Logan suspiciously. **You from Menagerie?**

"Have some more cheese," Logan said, peeling the wrappers off the cheese slices. Yump snapped them up and went back to the hamburgers. "Yump, listen, I know you've had a great day, but if you keep eating like this, you'll never be able to fly. The Menagerie knows how much you need to eat and how to take care of you. It's dangerous out here."

Bah, Yump muttered. **Yump just fine. Yump great at finding food. Yump take care of himself! Yump NEVER BE HUNGRY AGAIN!**

Something zipped through the air right over the griffin's head and clonked into the picnic table.

Logan and Yump both stared at it. It took Logan a minute to realize it was a tranquilizer dart.

Unfortunately, Yump realized it first.

BETRAYED! he howled. **Delicious cheeseburger TREACHERY!** He threw himself off the picnic table with a thump as Logan leaped to his feet.

Zoe's parents came running out of the woods in one direction; Matthew and Blue appeared from the other. Except for Blue, they were all carrying tranq guns.

RUDE! Yump shrieked, galloping in a wide, zigzagging circle. Despite his girth, he was astonishingly fast. He zipped by Blue, who threw himself at the cub and ended up face-first in the grass. Zoe's dad shot at the griffin again, but Yump dodged out of the way. He barreled toward Zoe's parents, trying to get around them into the woods.

Zoe's mom hit a button on her wristband, and a huge net flew out into the air. For a moment Logan was sure it would catch Yump—but then the griffin ducked and rolled right under it. He bounced to his paws again in front of Zoe's dad and veered off toward the parking lot.

Logan chased after him. "Yump!" he shouted. "Wait! We can get you burgers! Whatever you want!"

Nooooo! Yump howled, knocking over a grill with his wings. **Yump HATE sharing! All food mine all mine food!**

Zoe sprinted out of the restrooms shack and darted in front of the griffin cub at the parking lot. Yump skidded to a stop.

"It's me," Zoe called to him. "Remember? I gave you jelly-beans before anyone else did!"

Also gave it to brothers and sisters! Not nearly enough jellybeans for Yump!

Yump swung around toward the woods again, pumping his wings as he ran as if he was trying to fly. His tail lashed out and knocked over a trash can. He was leaving big lion paw prints in the dirt. Logan was sure his dad would be out here frowning in confusion at those tomorrow.

Logan ran back to the picnic table and pulled out the bottle of chocolate sauce. "Yump!" he yelled. "Look! Chocolate sauce! You can have the whole bottle if you come back quietly!"

Yump can have all the chocolate he wants out here! the cub bellowed, swerving around Zoe's mom and tearing toward the trees. **Yump FREEEEEEEEEEEEEEEE—**

A tranquilizer dart thudded into his thigh. Yump tumbled into a somersault and collapsed in a heap on the ground two strides from the woods.

"Nice shot," Zoe's dad called to Matthew. Matthew lifted his tranq gun and bowed like a conductor of an orchestra.

Logan ran over to the griffin cub and knelt beside him. The griffin's eyes were closed, and his roly-poly paws were flopped out on either side.

"I'm sorry, Yump," Logan said, resting one hand on the cub's head. "I didn't mean to betray you. But this is for your own good, I promise."

Zoe's dad drove the van up to the parking lot, and together they all heaved the griffin into the reconstructed cage in the back. Logan tucked the chocolate syrup bottle between Yump's front paws even though Matthew and Blue laughed at him.

"The last thing that griffin needs is more food," Matthew pointed out.

"He'll be grumpy enough when he wakes up back at home," Logan said. "At least now he'll have something of his own."

"For about a nanosecond," Blue said. "Until he eats it all."

"We'll meet you back at the house," said Zoe's dad, closing the van doors. "Zoe, quit giving me that look." Zoe dropped her eyes and shoved her hands into her pockets.

So they're fighting about something, Logan thought. *Is it me?*

And if it was . . . was Zoe on his side or not?

TWENTY-SEVEN

It took five of them to drag Yump's cage from the garage to the griffin enclosure.

"Yump?" Zoe said to Logan. "Seriously? That's the first name that popped into your head?"

"It just seemed right for him," Logan said. "Sorry it's not as cute as Roly-Poly."

Matthew laughed, and Zoe glared at them both.

DARLING SON! Riff bellowed, galloping to the gate as they came in. **Oh, NO! What is wrong with him? What terrible fate has befallen him in the perilous world?**

"Well, for starters, he ate all the food in Xanadu," Zoe said.

"And then we sedated him to get him here," Matthew added. "He'll wake up fine tomorrow." He opened the cage door, and Blue helped him lift the griffin onto the ground. Riff hovered over them, flapping his wings so leaves swirled everywhere.

I will stand guard until he awakens, he pledged firmly. He sat down and fixed his gaze on the red griffin cub.

"Just to warn you, he might be a little upset to be here," Logan said. "And his name is Yump. Squorp, don't you dare steal that chocolate syrup from him." The golden griffin cub jumped back from his sleeping brother with an innocent air.

ME? Would Squorp do that? He narrowed his eyes at Logan. **Hmm. Treasure for Clink.** The griffin swung his head around to where his bigger sister was crouched outside the cave, the golden bracelet carefully positioned between her paws. **Pirate booty for Clonk. Chocolate for Yump. ZERO BUPKES SQUAT for Squorp!**

"I'm working on that," Logan promised. "This is what I have for now." He crouched to slip Squorp the rest of the hamburger meat.

Cow! Cow! Cow! Squorp did a happy, prancing dance around Logan and nosed his hand gratefully.

Oh, Nira said, emerging from the cave. Flurp and Clonk were riding on her back, clutching her snowy white wings and fur. Nira eyed Yump's sleeping form. **Hooray. More of my children are back.**

Squorp! Flurp cried. **New game! Let's play Mom's a tree and first one to climb to the top of her head wins!**

No! cried Clonk. **Let's play Mom's tail is a snake and first one to pounce on it and kill it wins!**

Better idea! said Squorp. **Let's play Mom chases us around the boulders and the last one she catches wins and also Mom's tail is a snake so we all attack it as we run by and also if she stops running we all jump on her and practice flying off her head and also we are aliens.**

Yaaaayyyy! cried Flurp and Clonk.

Nira slowly, expressively, closed her eyes.

"One to go," Zoe's dad said, patting her side. "Don't worry, Nira. We'll find her soon."

Wonderful, Nira said. **I can't wait. With only five cubs I'll have far too much free time.**

Logan glanced back sympathetically as Mr. Kahn shut the gate. Riff was still on guard beside sleeping Yump while the other four griffin cubs dragged Nira off to chase them.

"One last cub," said Mrs. Kahn. "Any ideas, kids?"

Logan and Zoe and Blue exchanged glances. They hadn't yet mentioned the phone conversation they'd overheard in the school library. Logan wondered if Zoe would have to tell her parents about it now. Or maybe she already had, and that's what she and her dad were arguing about.

A piercing shriek echoed across the lake, followed by the sound of something slamming into wood. They all whirled around.

"The unicorns," Matthew said, bolting for the stable.

Logan and the others pelted after him. *Maybe it's the griffin cub*, Logan thought hopefully. *Maybe she snuck back in and is hiding in there—*

It wasn't the griffin cub.

It was Keiko.

The sixth grader was standing between the stalls cursing (Logan guessed) in Japanese and hurling apples at Cleopatra. One of her braids had come undone, and there were streaks of dirt along the sides of her face.

"Keiko, stop!" Mrs. Kahn cried. She jumped forward and grabbed Keiko's arm. "What are you doing?"

"Look what she did to me!" Keiko shouted, wrenching herself free. She pointed to an enormous rip along the sleeve of her jade-colored shirt and a corresponding tiny scratch on her arm. "This shirt cost seventy-five dollars! You do *not* know who you are messing with, horse!"

Seventy-five dollars?! Logan couldn't believe he'd heard her right.

"On the contrary," Cleopatra sneered, "I can smell you from a mile away, and you don't scare me at all."

"We'll see if that's true when I sneak in here one night and *eat* you," Keiko growled.

"You'd have to catch me first." Cleopatra tossed her head.

"What were you doing in here in the first place?" Zoe asked Keiko.

Keiko swelled indignantly. "I was doing *your* chores," she spat. "I was trying to brush these stupid albino donkeys." She pointed to the currycomb, abandoned on the floor by Cleopatra's hooves.

"I can't imagine where you went wrong," Charlemagne remarked drily from the other stall. "That's just the attitude royalty always looks for in its servants."

"I am not your *servant*," Keiko hissed. She flung another apple at the back wall. "And I am *never* doing this again." She stormed out of the stable.

"Well, then, mission accomplished," Charlemagne said smugly.

Cleopatra surveyed the rest of the group. As her cold gaze landed on Logan, he hurriedly bowed, and she paused to give him an approving nod.

"That one may stay and groom me," she said. "Everyone else is excused."

Zoe raised her eyebrows at Logan. "Do you know anything about grooming unicorns?" she asked.

"My crazy uncle once gave me a My Little Pony doll," Logan said. "That's about as close as I've gotten. Cleopatra, could Zoe please stay to advise me? I wouldn't want to do anything wrong."

Cleopatra sniffed. "Well," she said. "I suppose. This once. As long as she doesn't speak to me."

"I think I can manage that," Zoe muttered.

"I'll go see if Mooncrusher finished the repairs to the outer wall," Mr. Kahn said, patting Zoe's head. "Thanks for stepping in, Logan."

Zoe ducked away from his hand and gave him a sharp frown, but he left without responding to her look. Matthew and Mrs. Kahn followed, but Logan was glad to see Blue hop onto a hay bale to keep them company.

"Mom and Dad spent the whole day fighting," Blue said, yawning. "She says this is all his fault because of the hole in the river grate. He says it wasn't there during their rounds on Thursday or one of the mermaids would have seen it. She says the mermaids would rather comb their hair than do what they're supposed to around here. He says the griffins must have cut the grate open themselves."

"Squorp said they didn't," Logan said.

"He must be wrong. How else would it have gotten that way?" Blue said with a shrug.

Zoe led Logan into the stall and picked up the curry-comb, showing him how to rub in long, smooth circles along the unicorn's side.

"It's so frightfully, frightfully sad," Charlemagne said. He hung his head over the stall door to watch Logan. "Everyone will miss those cubs terribly."

"Hey, we already have five of them back," Zoe said. "We'll find the other one tonight. Or tomorrow before the agents get here at noon. I know we will."

Charlemagne stamped his hooves. "Five of them! Back already!"

"You're speaking to the girl-serf," Cleopatra reminded him.

"Oh, right." Charlemagne tossed his head and backed up with a snort.

"Cleo, are you ever going to tell us what we did wrong?" Zoe asked.

"It is so obvious, you should be ashamed to ask," Cleopatra snapped. Logan moved carefully around to her other side.

"So, the last griffin," he said, trying to change the subject. "How would you describe her? What kind of treasure might she like?"

Zoe shook her head. "No idea. She's quiet—a good listener. And clever; Matthew taught her to play chess already." She paused, twisting a lock of hair around one finger. "I've been wondering. I still don't think I left that gate unlocked. So *someone* opened it, and whoever let the griffins out must have done it for a reason. What if someone wanted to steal a cub? Maybe that's what happened to her."

"Like that Tracker," Blue said. He leaned back against the

wall with his hands behind his head. "The one who ran off with the Chinese dragon instead of bringing it here."

"We don't know that that's what happened," Zoe said, crouching to retrieve a fallen hoof pick.

Blue shrugged. "Of course people want to steal mythical creatures. Even the animals without powers would sell for a fortune on the black market."

Cleopatra blew out a skeptical huff of air. "Anyone who buys a griffin cub will learn to regret it." The unicorn sniffed. "Not that I care about your problems, of course."

"So if we figure out who let the griffins out," Zoe said hopefully, "maybe that'll lead us to the last one."

"Actually," Logan said, "I have a theory about that. But if I'm right, it won't help us find her."

"All right, griffin whisperer," Zoe said. "What's your theory?"

Logan hesitated. It sounded stupid now that he was about to say it. But what if he was right?

"I think," he said slowly. "I think . . . that Nira let her own cubs out."

TWENTY-EIGHT

"Ruh-roh," Zoe said. "The griffin whisperer has lost his mind." She climbed onto the hay bale beside Blue and leaned back against the wall. It was ridiculous how tired she was. She was too tired even to make fun of Logan's goofy theory properly.

"Wait, I'm serious," Logan said. "You can't hear the cubs, so you don't realize how they are with her and how tiring it must be. It's like nonstop insanity in there, and she's doing ninety percent of the work even when Riff thinks he's helping. Probably *more* when Riff thinks he's helping. What if she let them out because she needed a break?"

"But the cubs would have seen her do that, wouldn't they?" Blue said.

"Maybe she hopped out of the enclosure while they were asleep, unbolted the door, and then waited for them to find it themselves," Logan suggested. "She and Riff can fly in and out, right?"

"Sure," Blue said. "The fence is just for the cubs, or it's supposed to be. That's why we moved them in there."

Zoe kicked the hay bale with her sneakers. "Nira has been tired and irritable lately," she said. "But what kind of mom would risk her own cubs like that?"

Logan turned away and ran the comb through Cleopatra's mane. "Maybe she expected them to stay inside the Menagerie. Or maybe not. Some people aren't meant to be moms," he said quietly.

"Logan—" Zoe started.

"Hey, I know!" Blue interrupted, sitting up suddenly. "We can find out if it was Nira." He turned to Zoe. "The security tapes."

"There are security tapes?" Logan ducked under Cleopatra's neck and gave them a wry look. "That wouldn't have been helpful to check sooner?"

"No," Zoe said. "The cameras are on the inside of the enclosure; there's no shot of the gate from the outside. But you're right; we could see what Nira was doing all night."

"Let's do it," Logan said. He stepped out of Cleopatra's stall and bowed. "May we be excused, Cleopatra?"

She tossed her mane. "I suppose."

The three of them ran back up toward the house. Zoe pulled open the sliding door and led the way into Melissa's office, off the living room.

Blue's class picture from sixth grade hung in a silver frame above her desk; otherwise, the room was all straight edges, clear surfaces, and black and white colors. Melissa's to-do list for the day was printed out, with half the items in bold, and laid neatly next to her desktop computer. Zoe glanced at it and noticed enviously that nearly all the boxes had check marks in them. Zoe had gotten her to-do list strategy from watching Melissa, but she still felt overwhelmed and disorganized practically all the time.

One corner of the room was set up with the security camera video feeds and archives. Zoe sat down and pulled up the week's videos from the griffin enclosure.

"There are the SNAPA agents," she said, fast-forwarding through Sunday. The two agents zipped around the enclosure like windup cars. Logan leaned over her shoulder, frowning at the screen.

"Wait," he said. "Pause it for a minute?" He stared at the SNAPA agents and then shook his head. "Never mind."

"What?" Blue asked.

"That guy seems familiar for some reason," Logan said, pointing to the male SNAPA agent. "But I can't figure out why."

Zoe shifted uncomfortably and hit the fast-forward

button again. "Here's Thursday. There's me brushing all the cubs." She slowed the video again and watched the smaller version of herself finish another Harry Potter chapter with Flurp, then get up and pat all the cubs good night.

After she left, all six cubs descended on Nira at once. Their mother had been napping under one of the trees, but twenty-four paws clambering onto her back woke her up pretty quickly. She tried to sit up, yawning and blinking, but two of the cubs knocked her over and started wrestling between her wings. The other four began a mad game of chase that seemed to involve tagging Nira's head or tail every thirty seconds.

"Wow," Blue said, watching the screen with his arms folded. "That looks exhausting."

"See?" Logan said. "Poor Nira." He picked up Melissa's mug—a joke gift from Blue, which said I'D RATHER HAVE A COWBOY THAN A FISH-MAN on the side—and started fidgeting with it.

Zoe leaned her chin on her fist. How had she never noticed this before? Why had Logan spotted it in just two visits to the griffin enclosure? To be fair, whenever Zoe went in, the cubs paid attention to her—looking for jelly-beans, mostly—so she'd never seen them all focused on Nira like this.

"Where is Riff?" Logan asked.

Blue pointed to a corner of the screen. The father griffin

was flopped among the tree branches above the gamboling cubs. He was fast asleep.

"Man. When we get the last griffin back, we are having a family dynamic intervention," said Zoe.

"Talk to Clink," Logan suggested, pointing to the largest griffin cub, who was clearly herding the others into playing the games she wanted. "If she learns to play with her dad and give her mom some peace, the others will follow."

Zoe fast-forwarded slowly through the rest of the evening. Nira tried to give each of the cubs a bath and got thoroughly soaked herself. She tried to feed them dinner and had to break up five separate fights over who had the best or biggest pieces of food. Well after dark, the cubs finally fell asleep one by one. The last one was Squorp, who spent at least two hours bouncing out of the den to bother Nira instead of going to sleep.

At last Nira stood outside the cave entrance, looking at the little cubs all snuggled together in a big fur-pile. She waited five minutes, until she was sure they were all asleep. Then she backed away slowly, as quietly as possible, and settled herself into a pile of dry leaves. With a sigh, she curled up and closed her eyes.

A few moments later, Riff woke up, yawned, stretched, and jumped down to the ground. Dirt billowed up in wisps around his paws as he landed. He blinked at his sleeping wife, then took a step toward the slumbering cubs. Immediately

Nira's eyes flew open, and her beak snapped around his tail, yanking him back. Before he could yowl in protest, she shoved him to the ground and clamped her paws around his beak.

Riff gave her an injured look, and when she let go, he slunk off grouchily. Nira watched him sternly for a minute. Finally she went back to sleep.

And that was it.

They went forward slowly through the rest of the night. Nira slept like a log, and after puffing up his chest and pacing like a fierce guardian for an hour, so did Riff. Around two o'clock in the morning, Clink suddenly raised her head and swiveled it toward the gate.

"Look," Zoe whispered. "I bet she's hearing someone unlock it."

"So it's not Nira," Blue pointed out.

"I guess not," Logan agreed. "And that means it wasn't Zoe's fault, either."

Zoe resisted the urge to hug him.

There was a pause. Clink looked at her sleeping parents, then back at the gate. With a few sharp jabs of her beak, she woke her siblings. Her wings flapped and her paws gestured as if she was giving them a grand speech—probably about all the treasure in the outside world, Zoe guessed.

The cubs stumbled sleepily behind Clink to the gate, which swung open when she leaned against it. Then they followed her out, vanishing into the dark one by one.

Logan leaned over Zoe's shoulder again. "Wait," he said. "Go back. What's she doing?" He pointed to the littlest griffin, the one who was still missing. She trailed at the back of the group.

Zoe rewound a few frames and restarted the tape.

As the other cubs followed Clink, the little griffin looked around furtively and then quickly dug a hole next to one of the boulders. She shoved something into it, scooped dirt back over it, and patted it down. Then she hurried after her siblings, none of whom had seen what she had done.

"What was that?" Zoe whispered, half to herself. She brushed the screen with her fingertips. "What were you hiding, little cub?"

"It looks like she was trying to keep some treasure safe," Blue said.

"Which means she planned to come back," Logan pointed out. He rolled the mug between his fingers. "That's a good sign. Right?"

"I hope so," Zoe said. "We have to find out what she buried. Maybe it's a clue." She rolled the chair away from the desk and stood. Seeing the SNAPA agents on-screen had brought all her anxiety rushing back. They had less than twenty-four hours before the agents returned. At noon tomorrow, the Menagerie could be shut down. Worse than that, if they didn't find the last griffin, SNAPA might decide to kill her.

"Where are you going?" Zoe's mom called as they ran through the living room again. She was setting out plates on the table, which made Zoe want to scream. How could her parents stop for dinner? Why weren't they in a state of total panic? She had never seen them panic, not once in her entire life; but this time it seemed impossible not to.

"Following a hunch," Zoe called back, sliding the doors shut behind them.

Blue reached the griffin enclosure first and pulled the gate open as Zoe and Logan pelted up behind him. Squorp's head immediately popped up over his mother's wings. Zoe could guess what he was thinking even without Logan's power to hear the cubs: COW?

"Hi to you, too," Logan said, grinning. The three of them crouched beside the boulder they had seen in the video. Within ten seconds, all the griffin cubs except Clink had flocked to them, sitting on the boulder or poking their beaks between the boys' knees.

"They'd like to know what we're doing," Logan said.

"Wow, thanks," Zoe said, wrestling Clonk's nosy head out of the way. "I could never have guessed that. Ow, Flurp, you are too big to sit on my shoulder anymore." The dark-gray griffin cub snuggled under Zoe's arm instead.

There was a patch of newly turned-over earth where the littlest griffin had been digging. Logan started to brush it aside, and Squorp bounced down from the boulder, nearly skewering Logan's hand with his claws by accident.

"Okay," Logan said, sitting back. "You can do it."

Squorp scraped at the dirt, quickly digging a hole. He moved back a step as they all saw a flash of purple in the ground.

"No way." Zoe leaned forward and carefully fished out the buried object. It was crusted with dirt, but she recognized the pink, purple, and yellow threads underneath anyway.

This was her friendship bracelet. Jasmin had made it for Zoe two years ago, and Zoe had never taken it off until they stopped being friends. Even then, Zoe had still worn it at home sometimes where Jasmin couldn't see it.

The bracelet had gone missing a few weeks ago. Zoe remembered wearing it on a day when she'd missed Jasmin more than usual and then taking it off at the griffin cubs' bath time. The littlest cub must have nabbed it while Zoe was wrestling with one of the others.

Zoe's hand went to her bare wrist, and a horrible, sinking sensation flooded through her.

"Guys," she said. "I think I know where the last griffin is." She took a deep breath and met Blue's eyes. "I think she's gone to the Sterlings'."

TWENTY-NINE

Logan wasn't sure why Zoe looked like the apocalypse had just come to kick the Menagerie in the head. She was staring at the dirty woven bracelet as if it were, like, the epic tragedy of the century.

"So," Logan said, "that's . . . bad."

"That's *terrible*," Zoe said. "What if they find her? Of all people, the Sterlings!"

"Why would she go there?" Blue asked.

Zoe draped the bracelet over her palm. "Sometimes I talked about Jasmin and her house: the secret passageways, the hidden rooms, and all the cool and random stuff they have. I thought the cubs would like to hear about it, that's all. I never thought any of them would actually go *looking* for it."

"Is this such a big deal? If the Sterlings see her, can't you just zap them again?" Logan asked.

"Maybe," Zoe said. "But it's not really good for anyone to drink too much kraken ink. And seeing a griffin could trigger all kinds of lost memories. Plus, we never figured out what Jonathan was planning to do with the jackalope he tried to steal, so we don't know what they might do with a griffin."

"Whoa," Logan said. "Are you serious? He actually *stole* a— Okay, I have no idea what a jackalope is."

"Sort of a rabbit with horns," Blue said. "It's like the official mythical creature of Wyoming."

Logan blinked. "You're kidding," he said. "That's a thing? State flower, state bird, state mythical creature?"

"Depends on the state," Blue said with a straight face. Logan couldn't tell whether he was joking.

"Anyway, Matthew caught him sneaking out with it, and that's when we knew we had to wipe Jonathan's memory," Zoe said. "We couldn't trust him anymore. Ruby threw such a fit." She rubbed the bracelet between her fingers, brushing away some of the dirt. "What if he was going to sell it? What if they put the cub on eBay or something? We have to get over there right now." She stood up, shaking off griffin cubs as though they were raindrops, and hurried to the gate.

Logan and Blue ran after her. "Wait, we need a plan," Logan called.

Zoe didn't answer. She blitzed through the garage and was halfway up the drive on her bike before the boys could get their helmets on.

"This is not going to end well," Blue said, wheeling out his bike. "There's no way Jasmin will let Zoe into the house."

"Me neither, I imagine," Logan said. "But at least there's one of us she won't mind seeing."

"Who?" Blue shook his hair out of his eyes.

"Um, you," Logan said as they climbed on their bikes. "You could get into the Sterling mansion easily."

"Me?" Blue said, sounding genuinely confused. "Why?"

Logan hesitated. Blue couldn't be that dense. "You don't know Jasmin has a huge crush on you?"

"Aaah!" Blue put his hands over his ears. "Logan! Why'd you have to tell me that?" He hit the pedals and flew off down the driveway.

Logan caught up to him a couple of blocks later. Thick black clouds were rolling across the sunset, and thunder rumbled in the distance, echoing off the mountains. "Sorry," Logan said. "Do you not like her?"

"Even if I did, and I'm not saying I do, I can't date anyone outside the Menagerie," Blue said. "Or a human, for that matter. Besides, you're probably wrong. How would you even know something like that?"

"Check your desk on Monday," Logan said. "She lends you a pen nearly every morning, whether you need it or not. She talks to you more than to any other guy in class. She looks at you a lot, and drops things near you so you'll both stop to pick them up. And the other girls in class talk about it all the time—I can't tell if they don't notice when I'm around or just don't care if I hear."

Blue held out his palm and looked up at the sky. "So now you want me to use Jasmin's supposed feelings to get into the Sterling mansion and look for the cub? That's not right."

"But it's for the Menagerie," said Logan.

Blue sighed. "We'd better catch Zoe."

They found Zoe's bike stashed behind a tree a block away from the Sterling mansion. They dropped their bikes and helmets as well and ran up the road, staying close to the trees.

"Uh-oh," Blue said, nodding at the tall white brick wall around the Sterlings' backyard.

Zoe's sneakers were disappearing over the top.

"I guess we're going in the back way," Logan said. He had a horrible, uncomfortable flash of what it would be like to get arrested and then have to explain that to his dad. Another low grumble of thunder shuddered through the sky, like giant footsteps approaching.

"Zoe used to sneak in this way whenever Jasmin was grounded," Blue said. He grabbed the lowest branch of the tree beside the wall and hoisted himself up. Logan followed him as they climbed up through the wide, twisting branches and scrambled out to the top of the Sterlings' wall.

One corner of the backyard was a Zen garden with a smiling stone Buddha and water trickling over a pebble fountain. A shimmering blue pool, lit with underwater lights, filled most of the rest of the yard. Next to it was a small white pool house with slatted doors. An inflatable green raft shaped like a crocodile lay beside the pool chairs with a black towel discarded on top of it. *The pool must be heated if they're still using it in October,* Logan thought. He could see a black-and-gold book lying open on another chair, and he hoped someone would remember to get it before the rain came.

There was no one in sight, not even Zoe.

Blue dropped silently into the garden, followed, a little less silently, by Logan. It wasn't until Logan's sneakers hit the grass that he realized there was no way back over the wall.

"How do we get out?" he whispered to Blue.

"Zoe never quite figured that out," Blue whispered back. "Usually she got caught with Jasmin, and Mrs. Sterling hauled her home."

Logan shivered. *I really, really hope that isn't how this visit ends.*

They tiptoed across the yard, staying in the shadow of the wall, until they reached the side of the house. Tall windows, mostly covered by long, silvery curtains, looked in on a formal dining room, and through the cracks in the curtains Logan could see Jasmin, her brother, Jonathan, and their parents sitting around a polished cherry wood table, having dinner. A chandelier above them threw glittering reflections around the room, catching the gleam of mirrors, glass vases, and silver candlesticks. There were a lot of shiny-looking valuables a griffin cub might consider treasure.

"Over here," Zoe hissed from around the corner. They found her crouching beside a metal-and-glass door that opened into a room full of plants, surrounded by glass walls and skylights. Zoe cautiously turned the handle, and they all crept inside, ducking behind a thick palm tree. Logan knew that some of the fancy purple flowers hanging in the room were orchids, but he didn't recognize any of the other plants.

"Why is there a garden *inside* their house?" he whispered to Zoe.

"It's a 'conservatory,'" she whispered back. "I know. I used to joke that she lives in the *Clue* mansion."

"Maybe the griffin's in here," Blue suggested hopefully.

They split up to search the plants. Logan checked under the tables and poked his head into the thickest clumps of leaves. But when they all reached the far end, none of them had found any trace of a griffin cub.

"We'll have to go inside," Zoe said, glancing through the glass door that led from the conservatory to the kitchen. "Quietly," she urged, before easing the door open slightly and slipping through. Logan squeezed through the small gap after Blue.

The kitchen was enormous and immaculate, all silver and cherry wood, like the dining room, with black-marble countertops. Logan could hear silverware clinking and muffled voices from the next room. Jonathan said something that made the other three laugh. They sounded way too close, and for the first time that weekend, Logan found himself wishing he could be home watching TV with Purrsimmon sprawled across his lap.

Zoe opened one of the pantry doors and pushed the shelves on one side until they tilted into the wall, revealing a narrow staircase winding up in the dark. Blue went through first, followed by Logan, and Zoe came last, closing the door and shelves behind her and shutting out the light. Logan paused, getting his bearings in the dark. He felt Zoe's hand softly touch his back.

"It's okay," she whispered. "I'll take the blame if we get caught."

"Let's not get caught," he whispered back. "Where does this come out?"

"Jonathan's room," she answered. "Jasmin and I used to spy on him and Ruby sometimes, unless they were being gross." She gave him a little nudge and he kept climbing.

Blue was waiting at the top on a tiny landing. Zoe checked through a peephole at her height, then reached past him and slid aside a panel near their feet. They had to crawl through it on their hands and knees. Logan felt bulky shapes turn over under his hands, and something soft and heavy brushed against his head. Then Zoe opened another door, and he realized he was inside a walk-in closet nearly half the size of his whole room.

They stepped out into Jonathan's room, which looked as if its inhabitant was only crashing there for a night. A duffel bag full of laundry was slung beside the door, and an unzipped backpack with a couple of textbooks in it leaned against the bed, half covered by the kicked-off red, navy, and yellow flannel sheet. On the desk was a fat art history textbook, open to a chapter on Greek art, next to a laptop where a screen saver was rolling photos across the screen. Jonathan and Jasmin in the pool; Jonathan on a sailboat; Jonathan at the Eiffel Tower; Jonathan and a group of guys skiing; Jonathan and Jasmin playing tennis; Jonathan with a blond girl against a backdrop of orange and gold mountains and a clear blue sky.

Zoe grabbed Blue's arm. "That's Ruby!" she hissed. "I thought she'd deleted all the photos of them together."

"She must have missed a couple," Blue said with a shrug.

Zoe took a step toward the computer and hesitated.

"Forget it," Blue said. "The griffin is more important." He tiptoed across the white carpet to the door and peeked out into the hallway. Logan could hear the wind rising outside, as if mobs of leaves were rushing up to the clouds and back.

They slipped out onto a square indoor balcony overlooking the foyer downstairs. Closed doors lined two sides of the hall. An enormous round stained-glass window hung over the front door, and on the yard side a glass door led out to a deck above the pool.

Large pieces of artwork were arranged around the balcony; most of them looked like they belonged in the ancient Asian wing of the Art Institute of Chicago. At a glance, Logan saw stone dragons, tall porcelain vases, gold bodhisattvas, and hanging metal chimes. One of the doors on the opposite wall said JASMIN on it in pink glittery capital letters, with a sign taped underneath it that added KEEP OUT OR ELSE.

"I bet the cub's in here," Zoe whispered, padding over to one of the tall, skinny vases. She peered in, then slumped in disappointment. "Well, maybe she got into the attic." She headed for one of the doors.

"Wait," Logan said. His eye had immediately gone to a wooden trunk next to Jasmin's room. It was set up on a brass stand, and it had a brass handle and hinges. The wood was lacquered black, with white flowers and gold hummingbirds painted on it.

To Logan, it looked like a perfect place for a griffin cub to hide. He crept around the balcony, keeping one eye on the marbled lobby below, and crouched beside the trunk.

When he lifted the lid, a pair of shiny black eyes stared

up at him. The griffin cub ruffled her pale gray feathers and made a mournful, chirruping sound.

"Shhh." Logan put one finger to his lips. "We're here to get you out. Quietly."

Please, yes. The cub nodded and stretched her wings, ending with a shudder. *I don't like it here. Uncomfortable creeping feelings. Not warm and fun like Worry-Cub described.* She was the size of Logan's cat, but she looked squashed inside the wooden box. Logan reached in and carefully lifted her out, cradling her in his arms the way he'd seen Zoe carry the other griffins.

He turned and found Zoe beside him. Across the balcony, Blue gave him a thumbs-up from the doorway of Jonathan's room.

Logan felt his heart calming down. They had the griffin cub. Now they just had to sneak out the front door, and they'd soon be safely back at the Menagerie.

He'd taken one step toward Blue when the doorbell rang.

THIRTY

Reverberating chimes echoed through the house, and Logan heard a chair sliding across the dining-room floor downstairs. He froze, staring at Zoe. The whole balcony was visible from the front door. They'd never make it back to Jonathan's room before someone spotted them from below.

Zoe grabbed him and shoved him into Jasmin's room as Blue ducked back into Jonathan's. He caught a glimpse of lavender walls, white carpeting, an easel in the corner, two bookshelves stuffed with books, a couple of Monet posters, and an overflowing pile of stuffed tigers on the purple quilt on the bed before Zoe bundled him into Jasmin's walk-in closet. He tripped over a pair of pink high-heeled sandals and nearly knocked Zoe over; the griffin clutched him with sharp claws. They crouched at the back of the closet, under coats that smelled like Jasmin's flowery perfume, and waited in the dark.

Male voices greeted each other down in the front lobby.

"If it's for Mr. Sterling, they'll go into the library," Zoe whispered. "Then we can—"

She stopped as a door opened much closer to them. Through the slats in the closet door, they saw Jasmin come into her room and slam the door behind her. Her mother yelled something from downstairs, but Jasmin threw herself on her bed and didn't answer.

Logan stroked the griffin's soft fur, trying to breathe normally. After the encounter they'd had earlier that day, he could not *imagine* what Jasmin would say if she found him and Zoe in her closet . . . let alone with a baby griffin. Through his shirt, he could feel the cub's heart beating as fast as his own.

"Hey." Jasmin's voice floated through the closet door, and Logan realized she was on the phone. "What're you doing?" She moved over to her desk and turned on her iPod. A Leona Lewis song filled the room.

"Okay, wow, boring, Cadence," Jasmin said. She sneezed three times in a row. "Man! My stupid allergies have been going crazy the last couple of days."

Her bedroom door suddenly opened, making Zoe and Logan jump. A figure in a silvery pantsuit poked her head in.

"Jasmin? Did I hear you sneezing? Are you all right?"

"MOOOOOOOM!" Jasmin yelled, throwing a stuffed tiger at her mother.

"All right, all right, just checking," her mom said, disappearing again.

Jasmin got up to slam the door behind her. "So annoying. My parents are convinced it's tuberculosis or something. Listen, do you think Blue would come to my Halloween party if I asked him?" She paused, fiddling with a little glass unicorn on her desk, then exhaled dramatically. "I know; he never does. What are you going to be? Don't say a cat, because that's way cliché."

Zoe sighed. "We could be stuck here awhile," she whispered. "The only endurance sport Jasmin likes is phone calls." She leaned around Logan. He felt the wall sliding aside behind him and realized she was opening another hidden panel.

"Come on," she whispered, ducking through into the dark space.

Logan slid the panel back into place and followed Zoe down the narrow spiral staircase, carrying the griffin. Halfway down, a small window looked onto the yard. It was only about the width of a hand and a couple of feet tall, but through it Logan could see the rain starting to fall on the pool, the towel, and the abandoned book.

Zoe stopped him at the bottom. "Shh," she whispered, almost under her breath. "That's the library." She pointed to a small hole in the wall, and Logan peeked through it.

Small, dark-red walls stood on either side of the hole; after a moment Logan realized he was peering through a gap in a bookshelf, past a crystal dragon bookend. He could see only a tiny sliver of the room, paneled floor to ceiling with bookshelves. In his line of sight was a corner of a massive desk, big and solid like an ancient mahogany altar.

He started as someone crossed in front of the bookshelf.

"You sure you don't want any coffee?" said a deep voice.

"No, thanks," another voice responded. "I can't stay long."

Logan's heart felt as if it was seizing in his chest. He reached behind him and grabbed Zoe's arm.

"That's my dad!" he whispered. His vision of the scene where they got caught prowling around the Sterling mansion became instantly more embarrassing and way more horrifying.

"I appreciate you coming by so late," said Jasmin's dad. "I know you're on your way home, but I wanted you to see these." Logan saw him pass by again with a roll of paper.

"Wow," Logan's dad said after a minute. "You do have big plans, Mr. Mayor."

"Well, I'm not mayor yet," Mr. Sterling said jovially. "And of course I wanted to clear all this with your department before I make any campaign promises I can't keep."

"I can set you up with the right permits," said Logan's dad. "I can't guarantee anything, though, especially with regards to the people who currently own this land."

"Mostly it's mine," said Mr. Sterling. "So don't worry about that."

"Right. I'll look into which forms you need and get you an outline of how the process should work, which committees are involved and all that."

"I appreciate that," said Mr. Sterling. "You're new in town, aren't you? I think my daughter is in the same class as your son."

"That's right." Dad's voice was suddenly warmer. "He's why I need to get home, actually. He's expecting me. Do you mind if I give him a quick call?"

Logan's hand flew to his pocket. Frantically he passed the griffin cub to Zoe and dug his phone out of his jacket. He flipped it open and hit SILENT MODE a second before it started to vibrate. He could see Zoe's wide, worried eyes by the glow of the phone. Quickly he closed it again.

"That's odd," said Logan's dad. "Normally he answers on the first ring."

Logan crouched in the small space and tapped out a text. **Sorry. @ dinner w. Blue's parents. OK to stay over tonight too?** Guilt made his fingers feel heavy. But what else could he say: *Sorry, I'm hiding behind the bookcase right next to you, rescuing a baby griffin?*

He heard his dad's phone buzz and then his dad chuckled. "On the other hand," he said, "maybe I will have that coffee." Logan could see his dad typing a response to him.

No problem. Have fun, champ. Logan brushed his thumb across the screen with a smile before closing the phone again.

"Great!" said Mr. Sterling. "Now I can tell you all about the wonders of Xanadu, along with a few good reasons why you should vote for me for mayor."

Mrs. Sterling laughed from somewhere in the room. "I'm afraid that's the price of coffee in this house," she said.

Zoe tapped Logan on the shoulder and gestured up the stairs. They backtracked to the window and sat down on the steps, side by side, looking out at the lightning that flickered across the garden. The stone Buddha seemed a lot more sinister when they could only see it flashing out of the darkness every few minutes.

"Now what do we do?" Logan whispered.

"Wait till everyone's asleep?" Zoe suggested. "They have to leave the library sometime." She stroked the griffin curled on her lap.

Logan heard light thumping from Jasmin's room, along with a Katy Perry song. "You're sure she won't come down here, right?" he asked. In a flash of lightning, he saw Zoe smiling.

"Yeah," she said. "Jasmin's a little claustrophobic—she would only climb around back here because I wanted to.

She's dancing right now. She does that whenever she's upset. It cheers her up." She sighed.

"Seems like you miss her," Logan said after a moment.

"Yeah," Zoe said, but clearly didn't want to elaborate further. The little griffin sat up and climbed onto Logan's knees so it could peer out the window.

"Everything okay?" Logan asked, smoothing her gray fur.

Still creeping feelings. Like someone watching. Someone waiting. Someone out there hunting.

Logan shivered. He remembered that feeling from their close encounter at the library. Could the same person be here, lurking around the Sterling mansion?

What if it really was an exterminator?

He glanced at Zoe and decided not to worry her.

She rubbed the back of her neck. "So what's your dad doing here?" she asked.

"I don't know." Logan ran the toe of his sneaker along the edge of the steps below him. "I don't know much about what he does, especially since we moved here." Was it time for the awkward conversation about his dad's job?

But Zoe didn't ask any more questions. She gazed out the window, looking tired. "I'd better text my parents and tell them we're okay." She muttered into her phone as she typed. "Home as soon as we can. Hopefully Blue got out the way we came in."

Logan watched the rain restlessly. Something about

the meeting between Mr. Sterling and his dad made Logan think of the SNAPA agent on the tape, the one who looked familiar. Where had he seen him before? He felt like he could remember his voice having a serious conversation, maybe with Logan's dad. The square jaw, the thin eyebrows, the severe mouth . . . something about his face gave Logan the feeling that he'd misplaced something. Had he run into him around Xanadu? It couldn't have been back in Chicago. . . .

Logan's skin prickled like he'd just been dumped in an icy lake.

"Oh my God," he whispered. "I know where I've seen that SNAPA agent before."

Zoe drew her arms around her knees. "Really?"

"He came to our apartment in Chicago," Logan said. "Zoe . . . he was looking for my mother."

THIRTY-ONE

Zoe felt Logan shiver in the dark beside her.

"That means SNAPA was looking for my mom, doesn't it?" he said. "What if Mom knew something about SNAPA? Why else would that guy be looking for her?"

Zoe had known something like this would happen. The minute she saw the photo on Logan's fridge, she'd told her dad they needed to tell him the truth, but he wouldn't let her. She rubbed her arms, feeling queasy. Well, he wasn't here to stop her now.

"Okay," she whispered. "Look. I have something to tell you. But don't freak out."

Logan waved at the dark stairs around them. "I kind of

can't. Or at least, I'll do it quietly." She could tell he was trying to sound calmer than he was.

Zoe let out a long breath. "So, the truth is . . . we know your mom."

Logan didn't say anything. He put his head down on his hands. Zoe shifted nervously, wondering what she should do.

"Tell me," he said at last.

"I didn't realize it at first," Zoe said. "She has a different last name, right? I know her as Abigail Hardy. I had no idea you were related until I saw her photo on your fridge."

"*Oh*," Logan said, muffled into his hands.

"Dad said we shouldn't tell you yet," Zoe explained. "He said that if she never told you, then maybe we shouldn't. Or if she did tell you and you were lying to us about what you knew, we needed to figure out what you were up to." Logan jerked away from her, and Zoe reached out to catch his arm. "I knew you weren't lying. I knew you didn't know anything about what your mom does. I swear."

"What does she do?" Logan asked.

"She's a Tracker," Zoe said. "One of the best. Or she was, until she disappeared on her way to us with a Chinese dragon."

Lightning lit up Logan's puzzled face. "Is that the Tracker Blue was talking about in the stable?" he asked. "He said she ran off with it—like she stole it."

"I'm sorry, Logan," Zoe said. "That's what most people think happened."

"The SNAPA agent must think so, too," Logan said slowly. "When he came to see us, he asked all these awful, accusing questions as if she'd stolen something from her job and maybe we knew where it was." He rubbed his face. "She wouldn't do that, Zoe. She might walk away from me and Dad, but she loved her work, and she wasn't a thief."

"I don't think she was, either," Zoe said. "I don't think she stole it, and I don't think she left you. I think something happened to her."

Logan turned to look out the window. Rain pattered against the glass, and thunder rumbled like pianos being pushed across the sky.

"I don't know if that's better or worse," he said finally.

"The last you heard from her—" Zoe started.

"We got a postcard," Logan said. "Basically saying she had a new job opportunity and she wasn't coming back to us, ever. It was her handwriting, though." The griffin cub chirruped softly and wound her tail around his arm.

Zoe tried to imagine what she'd feel like if her own mother disappeared like that. Mrs. Kahn loved the Menagerie, but she loved Zoe, Matthew, and Ruby more. Neither of Zoe's parents had ever spent even a night away from the Menagerie and their kids.

"I didn't know Abigail had a family," she said, then

realized how that sounded. "But Trackers don't usually talk about their nonwork lives," she added quickly. "She always blazed in and out with cool animals and wild stories about how she caught them. I thought she was kind of this Indiana Jones free spirit." For a long time Zoe had wanted to be Abigail Hardy, although perhaps with a bit less dragon wrestling and manticore taming.

"She is," Logan said. "You probably know her better than I do. I've never heard any of the wild stories."

Zoe watched his silhouette against the storm for a minute. "I could tell you one," she offered. "Do you want to hear about how she brought us Captain Fuzzbutt?"

Logan leaned back on the stairs and stretched out his legs, letting the griffin flop across his chest. "Mom found your mammoth?"

"Yeah," Zoe said. "That's probably why he was so excited to see you. I think that's when Dad figured out for sure who you were. That, and your natural Tracker skills."

"I guess that's why the unicorns recognized me, too," Logan said, scratching under the griffin's chin.

"Matthew might have as well," Zoe said. "He's kind of an obsessive Tracker database; he'd know everything about your mom. Anyway, she was following rumors of another yeti in Siberia, hoping to recruit a companion for Mooncrusher, when she found this underground facility, and it turned out to be a cloning lab. So she knew she had to break in and see what they were cloning, in secret, out in the middle of nowhere . . ."

Zoe told the story the way she remembered Abigail telling it over the dinner table, with a tiny mammoth sitting on her lap vacuuming up all the spaghetti in sight. Abigail was covered in spaghetti sauce spatters, but she didn't even care. She talked like snowshoeing through the Arctic Circle towing a baby mammoth was the most fun she'd had since rafting down the Amazon with a basilisk strapped to her back.

Then Zoe told Logan about Abigail's adventures in Chile with the alicanto; her trip to Japan that brought back Keiko and the baku; and the practical jokes she would play on the mermaids, which somehow only made them like her more.

Zoe wasn't sure who fell asleep first. Pale, golden light slipping through the window woke her up. She opened her eyes, cramped and stiff, and found her head resting on Logan's shoulder and her arm around the sleeping griffin cub on his chest.

As usual, her first thought on waking up was her to-do list. But there was only one item on it for today: Get the last griffin home before SNAPA arrived.

"Uh-oh," she said, sitting up too fast. A blaze of pain ricocheted through her head, and she pressed her fists into her temples. "Logan, wake up. We have to get out of here." She nudged his foot, but he didn't move. She had to shake him for nearly an entire minute before he slowly blinked awake. The griffin cub stretched and yawned.

"She says she's hungry," Logan said, yawning as well. "She doesn't talk much, this one. Oh, she says she will when there's something important to say." He grinned at the griffin.

"We have to get home." Zoe pulled out her phone. There were about thirty text messages from Blue and her parents asking where she was. And it was nearly seven o'clock in the morning. "Oh, no."

Still stuck in the Sterling house, she texted Blue. **Hopefully out soon.**

"Come on," she said. She tiptoed up the stairs and listened at Jasmin's closet door, then snuck back down and did the same at the door to the library. Silence on both ends. She knew the Sterlings went to church every Sunday, but she couldn't remember when. Had they left already? Or were they not up yet?

Logan tucked the griffin into his jacket and zipped it up. A little beak poked out the top, and he nudged it back in.

Zoe stared through the peephole downstairs for as long as she dared, then felt along the wall for the switch that opened the bookshelves. The shelves swung out on silent hinges, and they found themselves in Mr. Sterling's private library.

It was always against the rules to be in here, so Zoe's jittery nerves felt entirely familiar. She swung the shelves closed again and glanced around. Not much had changed, apart from all the new campaign posters and handouts on the tables. She wondered if her parents were planning on voting for Mr. Sterling for mayor.

"There is a lot of leather in here," Logan observed. "And is that an actual lion's head?"

The griffin cub squeaked in outrage and started wriggling around inside Logan's shirt.

"Ow!" Logan crouched, readjusting the cub. "Careful with those claws, Sage."

Zoe paused at the door to the library. "What did you call her?"

"Sage?" Logan glanced up. "That's what she asked to be called."

Zoe tried to squelch her smile, but she couldn't. "That's the name I picked for her!" She reached into Logan's jacket and patted Sage's head. "I knew you were the cleverest cub."

Sage rubbed her beak against Zoe's fingers and chirruped in a pleased way.

The doors to the library were massive and wooden and covered in squares of dark-red leather bolted on with rows of shiny brass tacks. Zoe took one of the giant handles and pulled it toward her. She left a gap just wide enough to see the foyer and the front door.

Everything was quiet and still. The low hum of the temperature-controlled air, the polished white-marble floor, and the silent statues around the room made the foyer seem like a museum entrance right before it opened for the day.

The front door was only a few steps away. Even if they woke someone up when they opened it, they'd be down the street and on their bikes before any of the Sterlings made it outside.

Suddenly Logan grabbed her hand and stopped her. He put his finger to his lips and pointed up at the ceiling above them.

They heard a door close, and shuffling footsteps on the balcony overhead. Quickly they ducked behind the doors, and Zoe peeked through the crack between them.

Jasmin came down the stairs in her purple moose slippers, yawning. She was wearing a lavender silk bathrobe over a white tank top and the soccer-playing panda pajama pants she and Zoe had bought together. She rubbed her eyes and combed her hair with her fingers. She looked much less glamorous than she did at school—much more like the way Zoe remembered her.

Zoe had given her those moose slippers. It had been right after Zoe and Ruby had joined the Sterlings on a family trip to the Grand Tetons. They had entered the park through Moose, Wyoming, and Zoe and Jasmin kept cracking up at the name. They had thought up a whole behind-the-scenes drama for the park headquarters. Of course it was a moosical.

Zoe leaned her forehead against the wall. She missed Jasmin.

Jasmin padded into the kitchen and came out again a minute later with a bowl of cereal. She took it into the den right off the foyer, and in a moment they heard the TV turn on.

"She's up early," Logan whispered. "So now what? Run for it?"

Zoe shook her head. "The couch in there faces the foyer. She'd see us for sure. I guess the rest of the family went to church without her." She wondered if they could go back up through Jasmin's room and then down again through Jonathan's room and to the conservatory. But there wasn't an easy way out of the garden, either. And what if Jonathan had stayed home from church as well? That was something she did not want to find out by charging into his bedroom.

"Well," Logan started, "maybe if we—"

And then Zoe's phone rang.

THIRTY-TWO

Logan dove behind the desk as Zoe scrambled the phone out of her pocket. The ringing stopped. But so did the noise from the TV across the hall.

"Hello?" Jasmin called. "Dad? Are you still here?"

Zoe tiptoed across the carpet and flung herself under the desk with Logan.

They heard Jasmin's shuffling-slipper steps come into the foyer. "Dad?"

Logan held the griffin to his chest, trying not to breathe.

"Okay, whatever," Jasmin said. A moment later the TV came on again.

Logan let out his breath. "Who was that?" he demanded.

"And why wouldn't you put your phone on stealth mode for a breaking-and-entering mission?"

"My texts are set to vibrate, and nobody ever calls me," Zoe said, flipping open her phone. "Oh, Matthew. Of course. Idiot."

Immediately her phone buzzed with an incoming text message from Blue.

GET BACK HERE NOW, it said. **SNAPA AGENTS JUST SHOWED UP 5 HRS EARLY**.

"Okay, we run for it," Zoe said, snapping her phone closed again.

Logan could not see that ending well. "Or we call for reinforcements," he suggested.

Zoe shook her head. "Mom and Dad can't leave once the SNAPA agents are there. They have to show them the other things on the list—and keep them away from the griffins until we get back with this one."

"Not them," Logan said, taking out his own phone. "Blue."

"Oh, no," Zoe said. She reached for it, but he ducked away from her hand.

"We have to," Logan said. "For the Menagerie." He typed **CODE BLUE! YOU get over HERE now. Distract Jasmin so we can get out.**

No WAY, Blue wrote back.

Just get her upstairs for two minutes, Logan wrote back.

Borrow a book or something.

"This is awful," Zoe said. "I wish I could at least warn her so she can change."

There was a pause. Logan stared at his phone. Sage nosed her way out of the top of his jacket and tried to grab the phone away from him, but he held it out of her reach, waiting for Blue to respond.

RRRRRGH.

"Wow," Zoe said. "I think you actually managed to make Blue mad."

Suck it up, Logan typed back. ☺

"Poor Blue," said Zoe. "Oh my gosh, poor Jasmin."

"They'll be perfectly happy to see each other," Logan said. "She won't care why he's here."

"Maybe, but she really *will* care that she hasn't brushed her hair yet today," Zoe pointed out.

If that was true, girls were pretty silly, Logan thought. Jasmin's hair looked perfectly fine to him.

"Make sure your phone won't go off again, and get ready to run," he said, going back to the library door.

They didn't have to wait long before the doorbell rang. Blue might not have been happy about coming, but he came fast.

Jasmin paused the TV and came into the foyer, yawning again and stretching her long, thin arms over her head. Logan thought something about her face looked nicer than it usually did at school; maybe because her eyelids weren't all sparkly and her lips weren't too shiny. She got to the door and stood on tiptoe to look through the peephole.

With a gasp, she dropped back again and glanced down at her outfit. Quickly she stepped out of the moose slippers and kicked them behind the door, shivering visibly as her bare feet hit the floor. She ran her fingers through her hair and checked her breath.

"Oh, Jasmin," Zoe murmured sympathetically.

Jasmin fluffed up her hair and pulled the door open with a megawatt smile.

"Hey, Jasmin," Blue said, sounding more awkward than Logan had ever heard him before.

Jasmin let out a little fake yelp of surprise and wrapped the bathrobe around herself. "Oh my gosh, Blue! What are you *doing* here? It's, like, the crack of dawn."

"Sorry, yeah, um," Blue said. "Were you sleeping?"

"Of course," she said. "I always sleep in on weekends. And everyone else is at church. But it's okay; don't worry about it." She smiled again.

"Sorry," Blue said, staring intently at his sneakers. "Uh. I forgot my copy of *The Crucible* at school, and I was hoping I could borrow yours."

"Right now?" Jasmin said.

He gave her a charming smile. "I really want to know what happens."

She tilted her head at him, letting her long, black hair fall over one shoulder. "Blue. Come on. Is that seriously why you're here?"

"Uh," Blue said. "Yup."

"Even though you could borrow Zoe's copy a lot faster? And even though we read the last scene in class on Friday?" Jasmin arched one of her eyebrows.

"Oh," Blue said. He shuffled his feet awkwardly. "That was the last scene? Kind of a cliff-hanger, huh?"

"Blue," Jasmin said. "I know why you're really here. It's about my Halloween party next week, right?"

Blue's shoulders dropped, and he looked relieved. "Yes. Exactly. That. That is what this is. Absolutely."

"Let me guess," Jasmin said.

"Please," Blue said fervently.

"You want to come to the party," she said, "but you don't have a costume."

"Um," Blue said. "Sure?"

"Don't worry," Jasmin said. She took his wrist and pulled him into the house. "We have a *ton* of old costumes. I'll find you something great." She towed him up the stairs behind her. "Maybe we could match! I know we have his-and-hers bird costumes somewhere. Or, *oooo*, I could be Kate Middleton and you could be Prince William. Wouldn't that be amazing?"

Blue cast one last, panicked look around the foyer before

the Sterling mansion swallowed him up.

"Poor, poor Blue," Zoe whispered again. They hurried to the front door and slipped outside.

Logan took a deep breath as they ran down the long steps to the driveway. The early-morning air smelled fresh and clean after the rainstorm. Blobs of dark clouds were still scattered across the sky, outlined in gold as the sun tried to break through them.

They'd done it. They'd escaped the Sterling mansion, and they had the last griffin.

Now they just had to get her home before the SNAPA agents noticed she was missing.

THIRTY-THREE

Logan stopped to catch his breath as Zoe took the cub from him and settled her in the basket of her bike.

"Shouldn't we wait for Blue?" Logan glanced back toward the house.

Zoe paused as though considering what she was abandoning Blue to, but then she shook her head. "There's no time. If she gets Blue to put on a Prince William costume, she might keep him forever."

Fish-Boy will be okay. Sage sent out a reassuring wave to Logan. **House creepy, but dancing girl will protect him.** She opened her wings so the air could whoosh through them as Zoe took off down the street.

Good thing no one else is out this early, Logan thought.

They pedaled like mad. Logan thought of all the terrible consequences if they didn't make it back in time. The Menagerie shut down. Zoe and Blue moving somewhere else. Maybe even the death of the griffin cubs.

As they rounded the bottom of the Kahns' driveway, Logan spotted a sleek black car parked out front. With a last surge of speed, Zoe and Logan zipped into the garage and skidded to a stop.

"Do you think we're too late?" he asked Zoe as she picked up Sage. The door to the kitchen burst open, and Matthew came tumbling out.

"Finally! I was about to storm the Sterling mansion. C'mon." He charged back into the house.

"Where are the SNAPA agents now?" Zoe asked as she grabbed a jacket from a chair in the kitchen and draped it over Sage's head.

Matthew ushered them through the sliding doors and pointed to the lake. "Dad took them out on the boat to reinspect the water purification system first, but they should be back any minute. And I've persuaded Keiko to fill in with the griffins for now; but Riff and Nira were *really* not keen on that plan, so we should get there as soon as possible."

"You mean Keiko is— But she— Okay, you'll have to tell me how you managed that later." Zoe shuddered.

Logan glanced back and forth between Zoe and her brother, not sure what he was missing. How could Keiko "fill in" with the griffins? All he knew was that Keiko seemed terrible with the animals, and she hated dealing with them. He shrugged off the questions as he caught sight of a motorboat puttering toward the shore.

"Um, guys, I think they're almost here."

Zoe's and Matthew's heads swiveled in sync to peer down at the lake.

"Run," Zoe said.

They pelted across the road and down the hill to the griffin enclosure. Matthew hurried to unbolt the gate. As they slipped inside, Logan was overwhelmed by griffin thoughts.

This is an OUTRAGE! Absolutely unheard of! My grandsire would be molted bald in shame!

Calm down, Riff.

Nira was curled up against a large rock with the cubs playing at her paws. Riff was pacing furiously in front of them, his tail lashing.

I don't like it either, Nira continued, **but it's not like she can do anything with us both here. And she is an excellent distraction for the cubs.**

Fun!

Did you see this tail?

So fluffy! Best toy ever!

Warm and soft, too!

Play with us, Danger-Smell!

Can we play chase your tail and catch your tail and pounce on your tail and also we are aliens?

Logan stopped, puzzled. The cubs were all tumbling together, but it looked like there were six of them. He counted again—there was Clonk clambering over Yump to shoulder in closer to Clink. The black griffin cub was swatting at a fuzzy, rust-colored tuft of fur, with Squorp and Flurp poking it from the other side. But Yump was the only red-furred griffin of the bunch, so who was . . . ?

"Oh my God," Zoe said in a choked voice. Logan glanced at her. Her mouth was twitching, like she was trying not to laugh. Logan turned his gaze back to the griffin cubs as the reddish fur shifted and a long, pointed snout swung around toward them. Two bright black eyes glared up at them from below two gorgeous, tufted ears.

It was a fox. A very disgruntled fox. Its nose crinkled at the sight of them, and it sprang to its feet, shaking off the griffin cubs with a mighty wriggle.

AWWWWWWWW, the five cubs all chorused at once.

And then the fox started to grow, shifting from a small animal into a spitting-mad human girl.

Keiko.

Logan's mouth dropped open as Keiko angrily flung her braids over her shoulders, the sleeves of her white kimono flopping down her arms.

"I have never been so humiliated in my *entire* life. We will NEVER, and I mean NOT EVER under any circumstances, speak of this again. It NEVER happened. Do you understand?"

Keiko glared at Zoe, who still held the real sixth griffin cub.

"Of course," Zoe answered, all traces of her smile gone.

Keiko swiveled to Logan, her sharp gaze piercing. He snapped his jaw shut and nodded vigorously. Keiko stalked past them both, her nose in the air as Matthew opened the gate for her with a small bow.

"She was a fox!" Logan sputtered.

"Yes, Logan."

"Keiko was a fox!"

"Technically she's a kitsune," Zoe said. "You know, one of those Japanese shape-shifters."

"Oh, right, you know, those," Logan said. "No, wait. Never heard of them."

"Foxes who can turn into girls and back again," Zoe said. "It's more complicated than that, but you get the idea."

"Wow," Logan said. "That explains a *lot.*"

"I knew it was a long shot that the agents wouldn't notice, but it was the only thing I could think of," Matthew said with a shrug. "I'd better go make sure Dad knows it's safe to come in here." He vanished through the gate.

You found her! Riff's voice trumpeted in their heads. **My beloved daughter! You're safe!**

Zoe passed Sage to Riff, who nuzzled her affectionately before setting her on the ground and walking a full circle around her. His inspection was cut short by the five exuberant cubs pouncing.

Where did YOU go?

You smell like old things! What did you find?

Is it better than this? I bet not. Look, GOOOOOLD coins! I got them from a REAL, ACTUAL PIRATE!

Did you find anything tastier than cheeseburgers? Or did you find cheeseburgers? Did you bring any back?

Missed you!

Nira rolled her eyes, but reached over and plucked Sage out of the embrace of her siblings. She ran her front paws over the little gray cub. Then she nudged her back toward the pride, apparently satisfied that her littlest cub was unharmed.

"Everything seems in order," an unfamiliar female voice said on the other side of the fence.

"So far," added a deep male voice.

Those must be the SNAPA agents, Logan thought with a twinge of fear.

On the one hand, the griffins were back safe—but on the other hand, Logan himself was standing right here, in the middle of the Menagerie. He'd forgotten to worry about that in all the craziness with the cubs. What if the agents thought he was a threat? If they spotted him, what would they do to him—or to the Menagerie?

"Let's see how the griffin cubs are, shall we?" the woman continued. The door to the enclosure began to swing open.

THIRTY-FOUR

Zoe did a quick check of the cubs—all present and accounted for and playing happily. She wasn't sure about the rest of the list, but at least they'd finished the most important thing.

"Zoe!" Logan hissed. "What about me?" He looked around frantically. "I should hide!"

Zoe had stopped worrying about that once she found out he was the son of a Tracker. She figured that entitled him to be there as much as she was, although she wasn't a hundred percent sure SNAPA would agree. But before she could answer, he bolted for the cave and threw himself into the dark shadows.

Delighted, all six griffin cubs chased after him.

"*Ack!*" She heard Logan yelp as griffins piled on top of him. "It's not a game! Go away!"

Zoe's dad poked his head through the gate and spotted Zoe. She gave him a thumbs-up, and a wide smile spread across his face as he swung the door open the rest of the way.

The sleek figure of the male SNAPA agent was right behind him. Edmund Runcible reminded Zoe of a futuristic hospital. He was all cool indifference and crisp white lines against smooth dark skin. He held a clipboard in one hand, and his other hand hovered over it, gripping a bright red pen.

His partner, Delia Dantes, smiled down at Zoe. She had friendly gray eyes in a round face, large gold glasses, and long, soft black hair pinned up in a loop with pretty strands escaping from it. She moved in a quick, nervous way, as if she was always ready to catch someone falling out of a tree. Her vanilla perfume was just a little too strong, and it didn't quite cover up the faint burned-toast scent that came from one of the agents; Zoe had never figured out which, since they were always together.

"Playing with the griffins, Zoe?" Agent Dantes said. "That's terrific. Very good for their social development." She made a check in her small blue notebook.

"Come on in," Zoe said proudly.

Cubs! Nira called. **Come be inspected! NOW.**

Zoe watched the agents pace around inside the enclosure studying the six cubs and felt relief wash over her. She glanced at her dad, who mouthed, "Where's Logan?"

Zoe nodded her head at the cave.

"Ah," he said. "Agent Runcible, Agent Dantes. I'd like you to meet that new hire I mentioned." Her dad stepped into the cave and nudged Logan out into the light. "Nice work cleaning their sleeping quarters," he said, patting Logan on the back. Logan blinked in confusion.

"This is Logan," Zoe's dad went on. "He's working for us now."

"Seems awfully young," Agent Runcible said disapprovingly.

"He's precocious," Mr. Kahn promised. "Remarkable instincts."

Logan's whole face lit up.

"Well," said Agent Runcible, clipping his pen to his clipboard, "I'm sure you have the necessary paperwork filled out for him. I'll need to inspect that before we go."

"I'll call Melissa and make sure she has it ready," Zoe's dad said, unhooking his walkie-talkie. He gave Zoe a look that said *She's going to KILL me* and wandered away.

Zoe saw Logan tilt his head curiously at the agent, but Runcible showed no sign of recognizing Logan at all. She wondered if there would be any trouble once they realized his mom was the missing Tracker.

Well, too bad, she thought. *He's one of us now.*

"Do you have the soil-testing kit?" Agent Runcible asked his partner.

Agent Dantes nodded, and they went to take samples around the pear trees. As they moved away, Delia glanced back over her shoulder and gave Zoe a reassuring smile.

Zoe had no idea how they'd managed it, but she felt like finally the Menagerie was safe and everything was going to be all right.

Her gaze fell on Logan, now leaning awkwardly against the wall as if he was hoping he looked like he belonged. Okay. She had some idea how they'd managed it.

She crossed over and leaned beside him. "We did it," she said. "Well, *you* did it, really."

"Are you kidding? I never could have done any of this without you." Logan smiled at her.

"You know who we'll find next?" Zoe said. "Your mom."

Logan's smile faded. He shoved his hands into his pockets and looked across at the griffin cubs. "I don't even know where to start."

"Neither did I, when the cubs went missing," Zoe said. "We'll figure it out together."

Logan nodded slowly. "There's something else," he said. "We still don't know who let the griffins out." He flashed a smile at her again. "I always want to sing that 'who let the dogs out' song after I say that."

"I know!" she said. "It's been stuck in my head all weekend!"

He laughed.

"Maybe it wasn't anyone. Maybe I did leave it unlocked by accident," Zoe murmured.

"But Clink heard something at two a.m. Is there any chance it was Miss Sameera?" Logan said.

"I doubt it," Zoe said. "Blue is right. The intruder alarm would have gone off if she'd gotten in here. But we should figure out what she's up to and who she was talking to." Uneasily, she remembered what they'd overheard. Would dosing the school librarian with kraken ink take care of that problem? Had she seen anything besides the griffin cubs?

And how on earth would Zoe slip kraken ink to the school librarian anyway?

"Shipshape," said Agent Dantes, stopping near Zoe and Logan. "It's quite impressive what you've done in here. It feels like it's always been hosting griffins. I can't believe there were unicorns in here a little over a week ago."

Logan started and gave Zoe a wide-eyed look.

"I know," Zoe said to the SNAPA agent. "But SNAPA said we needed a walled space for the cubs, and we gave the unicorns a new stable, so it worked out all around."

"I suppose," Agent Runcible sniffed. "Delia, let's review the Aviary next, before the dragons." The two SNAPA agents headed for the gate, comparing notes, and Mr. Kahn hurried after them.

"Oh, right," Zoe said. "You still haven't seen the dragons. And I think you've really earned it." She turned to Logan and saw an intense look on his face.

"Zoe!" he said. "Was that true? You moved the unicorns out of here so the griffin cubs could move in?"

"Well, sure," Zoe said. "We needed the cubs to be enclosed, so we could keep an eye on them. Although that didn't work out exactly as planned." She snapped her fingers. "Oh my gosh! That's probably what the unicorns are so mad about! I didn't realize because they stopped talking to us about a month ago, long before we moved them—but that's when we started building the stable, so that's probably when they figured out we were *planning* to move them."

"Did you ask their permission or anything?" Logan asked.

"No, but they complain about everything no matter what we do," Zoe pointed out.

She remembered the tour of the enclosure she'd done with her mother a month ago, working out where the cave should go and how to relocate the new boulders for the griffins. Cleopatra and Charlemagne had stared malevolently at them from the far wall the entire time. And they had maintained a cold silence ever since.

"Oh, man," Zoe said, rubbing her forehead. "I really should have figured that out sooner." She was so used to the unicorns being grumpy that she hadn't thought they might actually have a real reason for once.

"There's more," Logan said. "I bet *they're* the ones who unlocked the gate for the cubs, during that moonlight gallop they do. Because if the cubs were gone, they'd get their enclosure back. Right?"

"But—but that's so thoughtless and selfish and, and terrible—" Zoe thought about all the heartache and worry and suffering the whole Menagerie had been through over the last two days. "And just like a unicorn," she said finally. "Okay, yes. That sounds exactly like them."

"Squorp!" Logan called.

The tawny griffin cub bounded over, clacking his beak, and leaped into Logan's arms.

"Hey, Squorp," Logan said, tickling the cub's chin feathers. "When you all snuck out on Thursday night, did you by any chance see the unicorns hanging around outside the enclosure?"

Squorp nodded vigorously. Logan listened for a moment, then rolled his eyes and turned to Zoe.

"He says Charlemagne wished them good luck finding treasure. And Cleopatra suggested they could swim out through the moat."

"I can't believe this!" Zoe said. "Those unicorns are eating nothing but hay for the next *year*."

"Or," Logan said, "you could try making them feel a bit more special."

Zoe wrinkled her nose at him.

"They *are* unicorns, after all," Logan pointed out. "*Unicorns.*"

"Obnoxious unicorns," Zoe muttered.

Logan smiled down at the golden griffin cub.

"You've been tremendously helpful, Squorp. And I've brought you a reward. Some treasure of your own," Logan said. "But you have to triple-promise me you'll guard it really carefully."

Squorp's chest swelled proudly. He smoothed his feathers and gave the enclosure an eagle-eyed stare.

"I know you will," Logan said with a chuckle. He set Squorp on the ground and pulled out his wallet. He unfolded it and handed Squorp a small photo that was tucked inside. Zoe caught a glimpse of Logan and his parents on the steps of an art museum, and then Squorp clutched it to his heart. He lashed his tail a few times, staring meaningfully into Logan's eyes, and then raced off to the cave.

"You're giving away all *your* treasures," Zoe said.

"Nah." Logan shrugged. "Getting to be a part of this is better than any photo or bracelet."

"I'm never letting anyone wipe your memory," Zoe said. "Never, ever, ever. I promise. You'll be working here until you're a hundred. Or until you get eaten by a manticore, whichever happens first."

Logan grinned.

And we will *find your mom,* Zoe thought fiercely.

"You should give Flurp and Sage something, too," Logan suggested. "A Harry Potter book and a puzzle box, maybe."

All the griffins suddenly stopped what they were doing and sat up, their heads swiveling toward the lake. Logan and Zoe exchanged puzzled glances.

"What—" Logan started, and Zoe shushed him.

Now she could hear distant noises, like bird cries and shouts. They had to be coming from the Aviary.

"Oh, no." What was wrong now? Zoe bolted out of the griffin enclosure. She glanced back and with a flash of gratitude saw Logan locking the gate behind them. The wet grass whisked around her jeans, soaking them, as she sprinted down the hill to the white dome.

Logan was right behind her as they burst through the air lock into the warm jungle of the Aviary. All the birds seemed to be freaking out: shrieking and tweeting and flapping their wings frantically. Zoe could even hear the giant roc, who was normally as calm as a puddle, bellowing from the other side of the dome.

She pushed through the hanging vines, following the sound of loud voices to the center of the dome, where Pelly's nest was.

As she got closer, she spotted dark red splotches and white feathers scattered on the wooden walkway. Her stomach twisted. What—

Logan grabbed her elbow and pulled her back. "Zoe," he said. "We might not want to see this."

"I have to," she said, and lifted the last vine curtain.

The SNAPA agents and her parents were there, all of them shouting at once. Mr. Kahn took a quick step toward Zoe, as if he wanted to shield her eyes, but it was too late. She'd seen everything at first glance.

Blood was dripping off the side of Pelly's nest, staining the pillows and silks. Feathers seemed to have exploded in every direction; some were even stuck up in the tree branches overhead. A bloody webbed footprint in the center of the nest was all that was left of Pelly.

Someone had murdered the goose who laid the golden eggs.

To be continued . . .

ACKNOWLEDGMENTS

Just like any wild mythical creature, a book requires a team to raise and nurture it—meaning we have a lot of people to thank.

Erica Sussman, thank you so much for your enthusiasm, wisdom, humor, and expertise at the care and feeding of temperamental authors. ☺ Thank you to Tyler Infinger, Tara Weikum, Erin Fitzsimmons (we love the cover!), Christina Colangelo, and the entire HarperCollins team, which provided this story with a beautiful design and spotless comma placement and which is now spreading the word far and wide about the Menagerie. Thank you also to Steven Malk, agent extraordinaire.

Ali Solomon, thank you so much for all your patience, hard work, artistic talent, and ability to interpret our notes—on how long yeti fur is or the shape of the Aviary—and transform them into wonderful images beyond our imagining.

A million thank-yous to the Newton Writers Group—Karen, Ed, Laya, Joan, Kathryn, John, Elly, and Mordena—for their patience, perfection, and perspicacity, and for pointing out ways to make Wyoming feel more like Wyoming. Thanks always to Dayna Lorentz for being the most wonderful willing reader and a great friend.

To our intrepid parents, who raised us in the midst of a never-ending adventure and a real-life menagerie of pets, including eight dogs, one nefarious kitten, a family of cannibal gerbils, six piglets, and two screeching monkeys (some of which were, thankfully, only visitors passing through the house). And to all our sweet, goofy, cuddly pets over the years, and all those of our relatives, friends, and coworkers whose anecdotal traits helped fill out the personalities of the creatures in the Menagerie. (Not that we're saying Maui and Yump have anything in common or anything . . . or that Sunshine is sometimes a soulful griffin cub, sometimes a melodramatic phoenix. . . .)

And, finally, to our lovely husbands and children, who patiently let us burn through phone time as we brainstormed plot twists, researched just how big a two-year-old mammoth might be, and certainly never got distracted talking about *The Amazing Race.*

Kari would also like to thank Tui for being such a fabulous and brilliant sister and an unparalleled writing partner. Working with you doesn't feel like work at all, which is the best kind of job. ☺

And Tui, being the big bossy sister, gets the last word, so she would like to thank Kari for being THE MOST fabulous and MOST brilliant (not to mention gorgeous, understanding, and ridiculously patient) sister with the biggest COOLEST brain on the planet. Could you cowrite all my books, please? ☺